Springtime
in
Summerfield

Springtime in Summerfield

Dianne H. Lundy

GRATUITY

Gratuity
Direct Number: 2134389957
(888) 290-0987
9350 Wilshire Blvd, Suite 203,
Beverly Hills, CA 90212

Published by Gratuity: 08/24/2024

ISBN: 978-1-965386-02-6(sc)
ISBN: 978-1-965386-03-3(e)

Other Books by Dianne H. Lundy:

The Girl from Nip 'n' Tuck, Part I (Autobiography)
The Girl from Nip 'n' Tuck, Part II (Autobiography continued)

Summerfield Series: (Fiction)
Summerfield
Return to Summerfield
Springtime in Summerfield

The Billy Allgood Story (Biography, property
of Louisiana Christian University)

(Available at https://bookstore.lcuniversity.edu)

Contents

"Catnip"

Lagniappe

Dedication

This book is dedicated to all the feral cats in
the world and those who care for them.

Introduction

Years have passed, and the adults in Summerfield have grown older. Their children have grown up and started their own lives and careers. Miss Betty Applewhite, Summerfield's unofficial matchmaker, is determined to unite a young couple who grew up in the town. She is an animal lover and supports several animal rescue programs, including the TNR (Trap, Neuter, Return) program for feral cats. She decides to use that as a method of uniting Jennifer Clark and Cody Hawthorne. They reluctantly agree to help, but excitement develops as cats suddenly begin disappearing around the town. The mystery deepens as two young boys are also kidnapped. Will Miss Betty be successful in her efforts? Will both the cats and the boys be rescued? The plot thickens as the story unfolds.

Author's Note

The "Summerfield" series is based on a fictional town and consists of various independent stories about the town's residents, who come and go. Each story has overlapping characters. For a more complete background on characters from previous stories, the author invites you to explore her other books in the series.

"*Catnip*"

Jennifer and Cody's Story

Chapter 1

A door opened slowly, and a short silver-haired lady's head appeared, barely visible, as she peeked through the space of the small crack she had allowed in the opening, her bright blue eyes scanning the street for any possible sign of people present in the usually quiet neighborhood. Seeing no one, she opened the door wider and picked up a yellow-striped cat, one of her favorite pets. She set the cat down on her front porch and began to shoo him towards a tall tree in her front yard.

"Go on now!" she exclaimed. "You know what you have to do."

The cat turned his head and looked back at her briefly. He resumed his path and reluctantly began to move towards the tree as she continued to shoo him. She was satisfied that her plot was underway.

That's my boy, she thought, as she pulled the door almost to a close. She watched as the cat, Toby, began to climb the tree. *Not too far, now, Toby. Don't go too high,* she silently encouraged him as he moved farther up the tree.

Confident that her plan was working, she closed the door and moved towards her home phone, which was located in her living room close to her favorite recliner. She picked up the phone and dialed 9-1-1.

"Hello, this is the 9-1-1 operator. How may I help you?" came the response.

"Hello. This is Miss Betty Applewhite. My cat has climbed a tree and can't get down," she stated.

"Miss Applewhite, not again?" came the reply.

"Yes, I'm afraid he has a mind of his own. He likes to go up but doesn't like climbing down," Miss Betty responded.

"Okay, I'll send someone to help you. Give me your address for the record," the operator instructed.

"It's 222 Quail Creek Drive," Miss Betty told her.

"Hold on, and help will be there shortly," the operator promised.

"Thank you so much," Miss Betty said, and she hung up the phone, smiling to herself. She didn't have much excitement in her life, but some was about to begin, once more.

Guess I managed to get the cat up the tree again without anyone seeing me, she thought. *I might be eighty years old, but I've still got what it takes when I want to get something done.*

Unaware that she had been observed, she took a seat in her recliner and waited for the firetruck and police car to arrive.

Jonas Green stopped trimming the shrubs by the side of Miss Betty's house as he saw the vehicles approaching. He pulled a red-plaid bandana from his back pocket and wiped his forehead, as it was a warm day. Even the large, wide-brimmed straw hat that he wore didn't keep him cool. Trimming shrubs always caused him to work up a sweat. Despite that, he always enjoyed working in the gardens, especially like now, in the springtime when the flowers were blooming, birds singing, and bees buzzing about the brightly colored blossoms. He usually kept to himself while he was working, but he had just happened to be trimming the shrubs at the corner of the house when he saw the front door opening and the cat being put out by Miss Betty.

Miss Betty, what you done gone and did now? he wondered. *So many matchmakers in this here town, and I have to work for one of them.* It wasn't the first time he had seen the firetruck and police car approaching, and he knew it probably wouldn't be the last.

He had been working for Miss Betty for the past fifty years, starting when he was just twenty years old. Finding work as a black man with little education hadn't been an easy task, but he was a good worker, and he found that he had a talent for gardening and growing plants. He had built up a business for himself, and with the recommendations of Miss Betty, a well-respected member of the community, he soon had more customers than he could handle. Now, at age seventy, he had turned most of the business over to his nephew, Adolphus, who had been working with him for years, but he had kept a few select customers, and Miss Betty was his favorite.

He watched as a fire engine and a police car pulled up beside Miss Betty's front yard, almost in unison. He wondered if it would be the usual people or someone different. Almost instantly, he recognized the driver of the police car. It was Cody Hawthorne, the son of the police chief, Jake Hawthorne. Cody, who was a carbon copy of his dad with blonde hair and blazing blue eyes, had followed in his father's footsteps and kept up the family tradition by joining the police force as soon as he graduated from high school.

The firetruck began to empty as uniformed fire personnel hopped out and surveyed the situation. They were all gazing up at the tree where the cat was stretched out along a wide limb, totally oblivious to the commotion below.

Miss Betty came hurrying out the front door as fast as an eighty-year-old woman could move along her front sidewalk. She was wringing her hands as a sign of distress and muttering, "Oh, my stars! That cat has gotten stuck in the tree again. I just don't know what I'm going to do about him."

What an actress, Jonas thought, as he watched the chain of events unfold. He shook his head and headed back around the corner, chuckling softly as he resumed his job of trimming the shrubbery.

"Okay, Miss Betty, we're going to see if we can get the cat down." The remark came in a distinctly female voice from the only woman in the bunch.

"Jennifer Clark, is that you under all of that gear?" Miss Betty inquired.

"Yes, Miss Betty, it's me. You know, you have to keep that cat inside. We can't keep making trips to get him down from a tree. We might miss an important call for a fire," Jennifer admonished her, speaking kindly.

"I know. I'll try to do better. He just slips out sometimes when I open the door," Miss Betty replied, trying to speak in an innocent voice.

Cody stepped forward. "Okay, guys, I'll keep the traffic away while you get the cat down."

"Sure thing, Cody," Jennifer responded. "Good seeing you again."

"Same here," Cody replied. "Now, let's get to work before a crime or a fire occurs."

"Guys, we're going to need the power ladder to get that high in the tree," Jennifer stated, as she estimated the height of the limb where Toby was located.

"Please be careful. I don't want anything to happen to him," Miss Betty pleaded.

"Don't worry. I'll take good care of him for you," Jennifer assured her.

Moments later, Toby was down from the tree and nestled safely in Miss Betty's arms.

"Thank you so much," Miss Betty said, as everyone began to pack up their gear to leave.

"Good job, everybody," Cody added, as he stepped forward to shake hands with all of the fire crew. His handshake with Jennifer seemed to last a little longer than those with the men, an act that was not unnoticed by Miss Betty.

The firetruck and police car were soon gone, and Miss Betty walked back into the house with Toby still in her arms.

"Well, Toby, we did it again," she whispered in his ear, as he flicked it back. "I'm going to get that Cody and Jennifer together if it's the last thing I do, and at eighty years old I probably don't have much time left."

Chapter 2

The firetruck crew rode back towards the firehouse with much comradery going on, most of it directed towards Jennifer.

"Wow, Cat Woman comes through again," joked Don Gates, one of the most seasoned firefighters on the force. "Nobody can work that ladder like you, Jennifer. Aren't you ever afraid of falling?"

"No, I'm pretty sure-footed," Jennifer replied. "I rarely lose my balance, and I'm not scared of heights."

"Good thing," inserted Calvin Griffith. "We can't have our star climber tumbling like a leaf in the wind."

"Ha! If I tumble, it won't be like a leaf in the wind," Jennifer retorted, laughing as she spoke. Her voice sobered as she continued, "However, we just have to do something about Miss Betty and that cat of hers. We can't keep going back to rescue good old Toby."

"You're right," Don agreed. "But you know Miss Betty and those animals of hers. She has cats and dogs all over the place. I've never seen such an animal lover."

"Yes, she's into fostering animals for adoption as well as helping financially with the rescues. She used to help with the TNR program in her younger days, but she can't do it physically anymore," Jennifer informed them.

"TNR? What's that?" asked Freddy Gillum as the truck entered the parking lot of the firehouse.

"It stands for 'Trap, Neuter, and Return' for feral cats," Jennifer explained.

"I see," said Freddy. "But why don't they just put the cats up for adoption?"

"Feral cats tend to live in colonies, partly for protection. Some of them can be adopted because they take to human company, but others are just too wild. They wouldn't be happy living inside. As long as they can get food and water they're content. The TNR program helps to reduce or control the population by keeping them from having more kittens. You see, a female cat goes into heat every few weeks if they aren't spayed or pregnant. That's why so many kittens are born. They're almost like rabbits."

"How do they know if the cats have already been trapped?" asked Calvin.

"They put a small notch in the tip of the cat's left ear. That way, they won't be caught and taken in again," Jennifer explained.

"You sure seem to know a lot about the program," Don commented.

"Yes, I never knew it was so involved," Freddy added.

"I've been reading up on it," said Jennifer. "I think I might like to do something like that someday."

"Well, no time to talk about it anymore. We're back at the home station. Time to get this firetruck parked and see if we have anything to eat," Calvin announced as he expertly backed the truck into its designated parking spot.

"Always thinking about food!" Don exclaimed. "Is there ever a time you aren't hungry?"

"Can't remember one," Calvin admitted. "Nobody can match my appetite. Whose turn is it to cook, anyhow?"

Everyone groaned.

"I believe that honor goes to Jennifer," said Don.

"You boys *would* say that." Jennifer sighed as she spoke.

"Cheer up. Maybe one of the EMT's has something cooked," Freddy said hopefully.

"Maybe. But they could be out on a call," Jennifer reminded him.

Freddy sniffed the air as the crew entered the firehouse quarters. "I don't smell anything cooking," he complained.

"And I don't see the EMT's," Don noted.

"Okay, okay. I guess you guys will have to settle for hamburgers. I really don't have time to cook anything else." Jennifer spoke as she washed her hands, donned an apron, and began to locate the cooking utensils she would need to cook the burgers. "How about a little help here if you guys are so hungry?"

The men washed their hands and proceeded to gather the rest of the materials Jennifer needed. One of them set the table. The topic of cats was soon forgotten with the prospects of food on their minds.

—◦◦◦✦◦◦◦—

Cody Hawthorne had driven back towards the police station alone, but not alone in his thoughts. He had known Jennifer ever since she was a young girl, as they had attended the same school. He remembered that she and her brother, Brian, had come to the school about midterm. There had been a lot of excitement when they were kidnapped by the principal's husband in a bribery scheme. The story had become a little hazy to him because it happened so long ago. The principal, Noreen Andrews, had been shot and killed while trying to protect Jennifer and her brother during the rescue process.

Jennifer and Brian had seemed to adapt well after it was all over. Brian was in Cody's class, and he had proven to be the brain child of the entire group. After completing grade school and high school, Brian had moved to New York, where his family's business headquarters was located. He had decided to become a lawyer, unlike Jennifer, who chose to follow a different path and become a firefighter. She was the first female firefighter on the force. Cody admired her for that.

That wasn't all to admire about her, either. He had seen her almost every week at church services. She was a faithful church goer, as was he. Sitting with his family gave him a good view of her sitting there so prim and proper. She had inherited her mother's Italian looks with an olive complexion, dark hair, and brown eyes. She also had great legs and a figure to match when she wasn't hiding them underneath that firefighter's uniform.

She was a little on the quiet side, and he liked that, too. There was nothing worse than an over-bearing woman, he had decided. He had met quite a few of them in his line of work as a police officer. Dealing with all kinds of personalities every day was not an easy task, but he liked the challenge. Meeting up with the firetruck crew to rescue one of Miss Betty's cats was one of the easiest things he had to do.

He grinned, thinking of how relaxed the cat had been, all stretched out on a limb, just waiting to be rescued. It was almost like a scene with the same actors playing the same roles over and over again. He had lost count of how many times he had answered a call to rescue Toby. *What a name for a cat! How had Miss Betty ever come up with that one?*

He didn't mind the rescues because it gave him another chance to see Jennifer, but what was his captain going to say if he found out?

He had the excuse of traffic control during the rescues, but there was little else he could use as an excuse for showing up at the scenes. He was supposed to be looking for criminals, not assisting with rescuing cats stuck in trees.

Before he reached the station, a call came in on his police radio. He was being summoned to another location where a fender bender had occurred. All thoughts of Jennifer left his mind as he headed towards the accident scene with lights flashing and siren blaring.

Chapter 3

Miss Betty had been summoned by Jonas to come outside and check his handiwork on her flowers and shrubs. She had one of the most attractive flower gardens in town, and both she and Jonas were proud of it. Over time, she had accumulated quite a variety of plants, with her favorite being the different species and colors of roses. She could never grow tired of her roses.

A little unsteady on her feet when walking in her yard, she was aided by a footed cane in her treks around her garden. Jonas was always on guard to make sure that his boss didn't accidentally fall. Her walks had grown shorter and further apart, but she still loved the outdoors in the springtime.

She took one last deep breath as she inhaled the scent of her favorite yellow rose bush. She then turned to go back inside, commenting to Jonas as she walked.

"Jonas, you've done it again. I don't know what I would have done without your help all of these years."

"It's somethin' I always enjoy, Miss Betty. I shouldn't tell you this, but you've always been my favorite person to work for," Jonas admitted.

"Somehow, I suspected that, Jonas. I wasn't sure, but I suspected it."

"Aw, Miss Betty. You sure know how to make a fella feel important."

"You are important, Jonas. Don't ever let anybody tell you different. I know it hasn't been easy for you, but you should be proud of your business and your reputation as a gardener."

"I don't like to brag, Miss Betty, but I'm just a little proud. My wife Eliza is always quotin' Bible verses to me, and she says braggin' is pride and a sin."

"Not when it's deserved, Jonas. Not when it's deserved," Miss Betty assured him.

"Here's my question for you, Miss Betty," Jonas commented as they slowly made their way back to her front door.

"What's that, Jonas?"

"Well, I know you have a lot of animals in your house—dogs and cats, I mean. How do you manage to take care of them? You need to be careful, you know. We don't want you trippin' over one of them and hurtin' yourself."

"Oh, that's all taken care of now, Jonas. I have a helper who comes twice a day and helps me with feeding them and changing the cats' litter boxes. She lets the dogs out in that little fenced-in part of my back yard right behind the house. She even cleans up after them," Miss Betty explained. "Besides, the dogs don't with me stay long. They're waiting for permanent homes. I'm probably going to quit the dog part after I find homes for the ones I have now. Then I will be down to just cats, and cats are easier to take care of."

"I'm glad to hear that, Miss Betty, but I think you need more help than just one person. Why don't you try to find someone else to help you?"

"I've been thinking about that, Jonas. I have just the two people in mind who would be perfect for the job. All I have to do is convince them of that."

"I think I know who you be talkin' about," Jonas admitted. "But I don't want to say, just in case I be wrong about it."

"You'll find out soon enough, Jonas. I'm formulating a plan right now."

"Well, here we be at your front door. Now you be careful, and I'll be back in two weeks."

"Okay, Jonas. I'll see you then. But remember, this little plan we discussed is a secret. Don't tell anyone else about it."

"My lips are sealed. Goodbye, Miss Betty." He waved as he walked towards his truck.

Chapter 4

Jennifer headed back to her house when her shift was over. She was renting the house next to where Cody's dad and stepmom lived. They had moved into the Hawthorne house when they married, but Jillian, Cody's stepmom, couldn't bear to part with the other house she had bought when she moved to Summerfield. So, they had settled on renting it since it was next door and they could keep a close eye on it and their tenants.

Jennifer had two housemates, as the house had three bedrooms. They were people she had known from school. All of them had different interests, but they got along and shared their meals together most of the time. They took turns cooking, and Jennifer was grateful that it was late, so the other two would have already eaten without her.

She walked in to find them sitting in the living room, watching TV. They had it on a Hallmark show, their favorite channel, which ran romantic comedy movies most of the time.

"Hi, girls. Anything good on tonight?" She addressed the duo, who looked up briefly from the show they had been watching intently.

"Jennifer, you're home late tonight," commented Donna Willhite, the most talkative of the bunch.

"Yes," added Laura Freeman. "We were beginning to worry about you. You missed supper."

"Oh, I ate at the station. You *know* the guys elected me to cook, but I fooled them by serving hamburgers, the fastest and easiest thing I could come up with at a moment's notice," Jennifer told them.

"So, what took you so long?" Donna inquired

"It was Miss Betty and her cat again. Toby was stuck in that tree in her yard. I swear, sometimes I believe Miss Betty shoos him up there on purpose, just to add a little excitement to her life with all the vehicles with flashing lights in front of her house."

"You got him down okay?" ask Laura as she tossed some popcorn into her mouth and chewed it slowly.

"Yes, no problem. He's very tame. Seemed to be just waiting for us to come and get him."

"Miss Betty certainly loves those animals of hers," Donna observed.

"Yes, she does. I've been thinking about getting into some kind of animal rescue program or the TNR program to help with the stray cat population."

"Say, that would be great!" Laura exclaimed. "You don't seem to have any other hobbies. I have my guitar lessons and Donna has her photography classes."

"Yes, you both have plenty to occupy your time. I seem to be at loose ends."

"So, why don't you call Miss Betty and see if she needs any help?" Donna asked.

"You know, I think I might just do that this weekend," Jennifer spoke thoughtfully as she pondered the situation.

Laura yawned. "It's getting pretty late. I think I'll head to bed as soon as this movie is over."

"Same here," Donna agreed.

"Well, I'm heading upstairs to take a shower, and then it's bedtime for me, too," said Jennifer. "Using that ladder is hard work."

Donna and Laura both laughed as she spoke.

"You know you love every minute of it," said Donna.

"Yeah, I guess you're right. Rescuing cats is pretty easy, but putting out fires, not so much. There's always danger when there's a fire."

"That's true! However, I know you're careful, and you have all of those good-looking firemen to protect you," Laura observed.

"They should pose for a calendar," Donna joked.

"Oh, come on. I don't think of them that way. They're just the guys I work with, not potential dates," Jennifer protested. "They're like my big brothers."

"Some big brothers! Are any of them single?" asked Laura.

"A few of them, but you two shouldn't have any trouble snagging dates. You're both good-looking," said Jennifer.

"True," admitted Donna, "but looks aren't everything. What we need is opportunity. Maybe we should throw a party."

"Say, that's a great idea," agreed Laura.

"A party…that might do it," Jennifer said. "However, we can't have it here. You know how the Hawthornes are about this house. Some parties can get pretty wild, and we don't want to take a chance on anything getting damaged or broken."

"So, maybe we find a public place," Donna mused.

"Good thinking," Laura noted.

"Okay, we'll give it more thought this weekend. I thought you two were sleepy. Plus, I still need that shower before I hit the sack," Jennifer reminded them.

"You're right. I can hardly keep my eyes open now. We'll be watching the rest of the movie, which has been on pause since you walked into the room. Then it's bedtime for all of us," Donna said.

"Okay, goodnight all. See you in the morning," Jennifer told them as she headed up the stairs. What she didn't tell them was that she couldn't get the image of one Cody Hawthorne out of her mind. Well, at least he wasn't a firefighter, so she hadn't lied about *him* being like a brother!

Chapter 5

Miss Betty arose at her usual time and set the table for breakfast. She didn't eat as much as she had in her younger days. Sometimes now just a bowl of oatmeal along with a glass of orange juice and a cup of coffee was enough for her. Plus, those foods were easy to prepare, especially with the instant oatmeal that she had come to love so much.

She looked around and saw four hungry faces staring at her. It was the cats, who had free run of the place, unlike the dogs, who were caged at night. They knew when it was time to eat, even though the helper had not yet arrived.

"I see you over there," she said. "I'll bet you thought I forgot all about you, but I didn't. Where's Toby, our king of the castle?"

Toby came strolling in, pausing to stretch as he entered the room. He was usually the last to awaken, but that didn't mean he wasn't hungry, too. He let out a "meow" as a morning greeting.

"There you are," Miss Betty said. "Let's see what we can find for your breakfast this morning." She walked towards the cupboard as she spoke. The cans of cat and dog food were lined neatly on one of the shelves, along with a supply of dry food.

She pulled out several cans of food and walked to the counter to open them. She smiled, as she remembered the old days when cat food had to be opened with a can opener. Some of her cats back then had thought it was time to eat every time she opened a can of any kind of food, no matter what time of the day it was. The new cans with pull tabs had taken all of the fun out of that game.

Before she could open the cans, she heard a key in the front door. She paused as she heard her helper, Gloria Howard, calling out to her.

"It's me, Miss Betty. I'm here to tend the animals. Sorry, but I'm running a little late this morning. There was a traffic jam on the way, and that slowed me down a bit."

"Hello, Gloria. I was just about to feed the cats."

"Now, Miss Betty, you let me take care of that, and you go on and eat your breakfast. I'll put the cats in the utility room and shut the door before I let the dogs out."

"Oh, my, yes. Be sure to do that!" Miss Betty exclaimed.

"I'll never forget the first time I was here. I made the mistake of bringing the dogs through the kitchen where the cats were eating. What a catastrophe!"

They both started laughing, remembering the scene that had resembled a comedy show.

"There were dogs barking and cats hissing and jumping on top of the cabinets," said Miss Betty.

"Yes, and the cat food was all over the place when the dogs went after it. I thought I would never get it cleaned up." Gloria shook her head as she spoke. "I certainly learned my lesson."

"Right, and don't let the dogs around food if you don't plan to feed them," Miss Betty reminded her.

Sometime later, with breakfast over and all the animals fed and tended to, Gloria finished washing the breakfast dishes while Miss Betty settled in her favorite chair to look over the morning paper that Gloria had picked up for her on the way into the house.

The dogs were in a spare room that opened into the living room with a baby gate keeping them contained. They soon settled down for a morning nap in their beds. The cats, who had each had picked out a favorite spot to nap, followed suit, leaving Miss Betty to enjoy the peace and quiet as she turned through the pages of the paper.

The phone rang unexpectedly, breaking the silence that had fallen upon the group. Miss Betty reached for the unit located next to her chair, wondering who could be calling her so early on a Saturday morning.

"Hello," she said speaking rather loudly into the receiver. Her hearing wasn't what it used to be.

"Miss Betty, this is Jennifer Clark. I would like to talk to you about your animal rescue operation and see if there's any way I could be of help to you."

Miss Betty almost reeled from shock. It looked like her plan just might be underway, and she hadn't even had to try very hard. She thought for a minute before she replied.

"Jennifer, that's so kind of you. I can always use some help, and I was just thinking about getting someone to lend me an extra hand. You called just in time. Why don't you come over after lunch and we'll talk about it?"

"That sounds like a good idea. What time should I be there?" Jennifer asked.

"Let's say about one o'clock. I think that should give us plenty of time to go over some things before it's time to feed the animals again," Miss Betty told her.

"Great. I'll see you then," Jennifer agreed.

Gloria's duties also included feeding Miss Betty. Breakfast took care of itself, but Gloria usually prepared some kind of light lunch and left it in the refrigerator. Sometimes it was a salad, and sometimes it was a sandwich. It didn't take much to feed Miss Betty these days. She had solved the problem of the nighttime meal by cooking a week's worth of foods that could be heated in the microwave. She dished the food into microwave-proof plates with sealed lids and stored them in the refrigerator. Mondays were her days to cook, so she didn't have to stay late today.

She let the dogs out one more time, fastening leashes onto their collars before entering the living room. The cats, who were used to the routine, barely looked up from their naps. There was no food to fight over now. After she brought the dogs back and secured them in their room, she took her leave, informing Miss Betty that she had left a tasty salad in the refrigerator.

Miss Betty was somewhat relieved that nobody else would be there while she and Jennifer had their chat. As lunchtime approached, she headed for the kitchen and removed the salad from the refrigerator, pouring herself a glass of iced tea to go with it. She sat at the small dining table, eating the salad slowly and thinking about the best way to approach the subject of Jennifer's offer to help. She already had a fairly good idea of what she wanted Jennifer to do, and it was going to take at least two people to do it. Plus, she knew just the person who would be the perfect partner for Jennifer. Her plan was definitely coming together.

22

Chapter 6

Jennifer arrived promptly at one o'clock. Miss Betty was waiting for her and didn't take long answering the doorbell. She invited Jennifer to come and sit in the living room while they discussed exactly what Jennifer could do to help her.

Jennifer looked around, amazed at the number of napping cats. The two dogs in the other room didn't escape her notice, either. They had roused at the sound of the doorbell and were barking at the sight of a stranger in the house.

"Quiet, now, you dogs!" Miss Betty instructed. "Alfred, Georgia, go back to sleep."

The dogs immediately stopped barking and headed back to their beds.

"Gee, Miss Betty. You certainly have them trained. I didn't realize you took care of so many animals at the same time!" she exclaimed. "But tell me, how do you keep the cats so calm through all the ruckus?"

"Well, I have my little tricks," Miss Betty admitted. "If they get too rowdy, I just throw a few toys filled with catnip around on the floor.

They love it, and it calms them down after a little while. Then, they're usually ready for a nap."

"Catnip, huh? I've heard of that. I just never quite knew how it worked."

"Oh, it doesn't work on every cat or the same way on every cat, but if you can get most of them occupied with the toys, the rest of them will calm down. I don't have as many animals as I used to have. Toby is a permanent resident. He was a rescue cat, but we seemed to hit it off so well that I decided to keep him. We were both lonely, and I guess the good Lord just brought us together at the right time."

"Yes, if you could just keep him inside, it would be a big help to everyone," Jennifer said, chuckling as she spoke.

"I hope to do that from now on. I apologize for having to call on your departments so often," Miss Betty told her."

"So, you're not keeping the other animals permanently?" Jennifer inquired.

"No, these are my last two dogs. They're both sweet, and I think I've found homes for them. I have some people coming by tomorrow afternoon to look at them. I plan to re-home those other cats, too. Then it will be just Toby and me. I might keep one or two cats as company for him."

"So, what do you need me for?" Jennifer asked, with a puzzled look on her face.

"Have you heard of the TNR program?"

"Yes, I've been reading up on it," said Jennifer.

"I used to participate in it quite literally, staking out the cats to trap. Now, at my age I can't do that anymore. The last people who were helping me moved, and I need to turn the program over to someone else. I can see that you love cats by the way you take care of Toby every time you bring him down from that tree."

"Yes, Toby!" Jennifer exclaimed. "He is lovable."

"I can fill you in on the details of exactly what you do. I have all of the equipment in my garage except for the food you need to put in the traps. There's just one more thing I should tell you before you agree to join the program."

"What's that?" asked Jennifer.

"It's a pretty hard job for just one person because you can be out there a long time. The best time to trap the cats is dusk or dawn, and I wouldn't feel that you were safe all alone these days. So, you'll need a partner. Preferably a male."

"Did you have anybody special in mind?" Jennifer inquired.

"As a matter of fact, I do. What about Cody Hawthorne? He's always so helpful with getting Toby out of that tree. He seems to like cats."

"Cody…well, I don't know. He has a pretty busy schedule, being a police officer."

"Even police officers get time off. Why don't I give him a call?"

"I guess it wouldn't hurt to try. The worst he can do is say, 'No.'" Jennifer considered the situation.

"You're right, but somehow, I think he just might say, 'Yes.'"

"Do you really think so?" Jennifer asked with a slight sign hint of hope in her voice.

"I'm a pretty good judge of people now that I'm eighty years old. How could he refuse a request from a little old lady?"

"Miss Betty, you are a sneaky one! Okay, I'll let *you* call him, and you can call me with the results."

"It's a deal. I'll get right on that phone call tonight."

"Okay. Well, if that's all we can do for now, I guess I'll head out. I need to run some errands. I'll be waiting for your call," Jennifer told her.

"Keep your fingers crossed. I'll call you as soon as I know anything," Miss Betty replied as she rose to walk Jennifer to the front door. She let

Jennifer out and then closed the door slowly, formulating a speech for her call to Cody. Her plan to get those two together just had to work! They would make a perfect couple, she had decided. She would pray about it and hope that God would agree with her idea.

Jennifer felt like skipping down the sidewalk as she left. Her heart was beating just a little faster as she thought of working with Cody. He was friendly enough and always spoke kindly to her whenever they met at church or on one of Toby's rescues. But would he be willing to devote so much time to the rescue of feral cats? She would just have to wait for that phone call to find out. In the meantime, she was not going to mention it to her housemates, she decided. They were already excited about planning that party they had discussed. She wasn't much of a party goer, but she would have to put in an appearance at that one.

Chapter 7

Miss Betty wasted no time phoning Cody that night. She had her speech all planned. She just hoped Cody would accept her invitation to help her with the TNR program. It definitely needed some new members to keep it going. It was time to pass the torch on to someone younger and sprier than she was. She hadn't actually been out on a trapping expedition in quite some time. She missed it but realized that it was now beyond her physical capabilities to chase down stray cats.

She had gotten Cody's cell phone number from his stepmom, Jillian, who was a member of her Bible study group. She had explained that she had a job that she needed help with and that Cody seemed like the perfect person to help her.

Cody answered the call after the first ring. He was surprised to hear Miss Betty's voice. He wondered why she would be calling him at this hour. Surely, Toby wasn't up in tree again at night. Plus, he was off duty now, so he couldn't help with that problem.

She quickly explained the situation to Cody, telling him that she was restarting the TNR program and that she needed some younger people to take over the trapping and transport of the feral cats to the vet. She said that she knew he must love animals because he always showed up to rescue Toby when he was stuck in a tree.

"Well, I don't know, Miss Betty," he said. "I don't always have a regular schedule, being a police officer."

"You have some free days, don't you?" she persisted.

"Yes, most of the time unless some emergency comes up. I'm usually free on the weekends."

"That's great!" Miss Betty exclaimed. "However, the cats should be taken to the vet as soon as possible because they have to stay in the cage until they get to the vet's office. Why don't you come over to my house and meet your partner and we can discuss it?"

"When would be a good time for that?" he inquired.

"How about Tuesday night? Are you free then?" she asked.

"Yes, I'm working the day shifts now, so Tuesday night will be fine."

"Okay. Let's make it for 7 p.m. That should give you plenty of time to eat, shower, and change clothes."

"Sounds like a plan to me. But tell me, who's my partner?"

"It's a surprise, but one I think you'll like," Miss Betty told him.

"Miss Betty, you're always up to something! Don't be pairing me up with somebody I won't like."

"Oh, no worries about that. Just trust me and show up on time."

"Okay, Miss Betty. I'll see you then," he promised.

What could Miss Betty have up her sleeve now? She has a reputation for being one of the biggest matchmakers in town. Most likely, she had some girl picked out for him and was trying to get them together, he decided. Well, he might as well go and get it over with. He just hoped it wouldn't be somebody he didn't couldn't get along with.

Miss Betty promptly called Jennifer and told her that Cody had agreed to come to her house on Tuesday night to learn more about the TNR program.

"I told him to be here at 7 p.m., so can you make it then?" Miss Betty asked Jennifer.

"Yes, I can be there. I just hope Cody isn't too disappointed in having me as his partner."

"Oh, I think it will work out just fine," Miss Betty assured her. "All you need to do is show up and look pretty."

"Look pretty, huh? I guess I can try. I'll see you then," Jennifer said, and she touched her cell phone to end the call.

She supposed it was about time to break the news to her housemates. She would have to endure some kidding, but it would be worth it if everything worked out with both her, Cody, and the cat trapping program. She just hoped they would be successful and could carry on Miss Betty's legacy.

She broke the news to them Tuesday over their evening meal. Instead of teasing, she was surprised to be met with a touch of jealousy from her housemates.

"I can't believe you lucked out and are going to be working with Cody Hawthorne, one of the best-looking cops on the Summerfield force," Donna lamented.

"Yes, and we haven't even had our party yet," Laura added.

"Well, cheer up. I have an idea for the party," Jennifer told them.

"What?" they asked in unison.

"Why don't we make it a fundraiser to collect money for the TNR program and also for fostering homeless cats?" Jennifer asked.

"Well, it's a start," said Donna. "But how would we go about it?"

"First, we have to make it fun," said Jennifer. "We get a band, get some party food donations, and sell tickets for admission. But we have to find a place big enough to hold a crowd, hopefully one that will donate the space to a good cause."

"Hmm… that could work," mused Laura. "How much time would we need to set it up?"

"I don't really know. I would say several months. Plus, we need advertisement to sell the tickets."

"The radio station does free ads for worthy causes. Plus, we could use Facebook," said Donna.

"Great. That's a start. I'm leaving it to you two girls to get everything going. Laura, you start looking for a place to hold the party, and Donna, you inquire about a radio ad, come up with an ad for Facebook, and also get some flyers printed to place around town. Plus, we need to decide on a price for the tickets and get someone to print them for us."

"Okay, we'll work on that while you're out hunting cats with Cody," said Laura.

"That's if he still agrees to do it after he sees who his partner will be," Jennifer reminded them.

"Oh, I have no doubt that he will agree," Donna exclaimed. "Girl, you just have no self-confidence. You have us all beat when it comes to looks."

"She's right. We are a little jealous, but you're so lovable we can't be jealous for long," Laura admitted.

"I never really thought about it. I spend most of my waking hours wearing firefighters' clothes," Jennifer told them.

"Just find something else to wear tonight," Donna advised. "Make the guy notice you."

"Yes, let your true beauty shine through," said Laura.

"Okay, okay. I get it. I'll see what I can come up with that doesn't look too enticing. You two can do the dishes if you don't mind. I need to get ready for my meeting," Jennifer decided.

"Sure thing," said Donna.

"Pick out a good outfit," Laura raised her voice to follow Jennifer, who was climbing the stairs to her bedroom.

Jennifer had settled on a yellow sundress complemented by gold hoop earrings and a gold heart-shaped necklace. She slipped on some white sandals and picked up a light-weight white shawl on her way out, just in case the evening turned chilly. It was still early spring, and the hot weather had not set in yet.

She stopped a moment before exiting to give her housemates a glimpse of her outfit.

"Good job, girl," Donna told her.

"Cody can hardly refuse now," added Laura.

"Thanks for the input. I'll see what happens," Jennifer said as she exited the door and headed for her car.

As she drove to Miss Betty's house, Jennifer wished it wasn't too dark to admire the flowers along the way. Summerfield was really a beautiful town, and people took good care of their yards. Miss Betty's garden was one of the best, and it was a shame she wouldn't be able to walk though it tonight. Oh, well, there would be plenty of time for that, she reasoned. She would probably be spending a lot of time at Miss Betty's house. It all depended on Cody and what he thought of the TNR program and of pairing up with her to trap the cats.

Chapter 8

Cody was on his way to Miss Betty's house. It was the first time he was going there at night and the first time he was going in his own vehicle, a shiny new Chevy truck, instead of in a police car. He felt his palms beginning to sweat as he gripped the steering wheel. It had been a while since he had been paired up with a woman. He wondered who Miss Betty had picked for his partner. He felt almost like turning the truck around and heading back to his apartment, but he couldn't let Miss Betty down. Everybody in town loved Miss Betty, and he would never live it down if word got around that he had chickened out on one of her most beloved projects. He swallowed hard and rubbed his hands over his pants, one at a time, as he approached Miss Betty's house. He could see a car parked out in front of the house. He recognized it as belonging to Jennifer Clark, as he had seen her driving it to church.

He began to relax a little. At least it was somebody he already knew, and a really pretty woman at that. In fact, Jennifer was one of the prettiest women he'd ever seen. Why hadn't he thought about that before now? Great, now his palms were beginning to sweat again.

He walked up the sidewalk and rang the doorbell. He was surprised when Jennifer opened it instead of Miss Betty.

"Cody, come in," she greeted him pleasantly.

"Yes, Cody, we're so glad you decided to come," added Miss Betty, who was sitting in her recliner with Toby in her lap.

Cody looked around at the array of cats who had stationed themselves at their favorite spots in the room. Miss Betty had provided a number of cat beds and also some climbing towers with a place to sleep on the top.

"What a lot of cats you have," he said.

"Oh, I'm not keeping all of them. Most of them are fosters," Miss Betty commented.

"You should have been here last week," Jennifer interjected. "She had two dogs who were like burglar alarms. They barked every time the doorbell rang."

"Where are they now?" Cody asked.

"Oh, they have their forever homes. Two families came by Sunday afternoon and just fell in love with them right away. The feeling was mutual. You see that barricade over there in the door? That was their room. I'm going to have my helper, Gloria, clean it out for me. I'm out of the dog business. It's just cats for me from now on," Miss Betty said.

"So, you're giving up all of the cats except Toby?" Cody inquired.

"Well, I was going to, but I have decided to keep two of them as company for Toby. One is that tuxedo cat over there. Her name is Orphan Annie. Somebody found her when she was just a kitten. She was hiding under a dumpster. The vet I use asked me if I would take her, so how could I refuse? The other one is that snow white cat with green eyes. I named her Snowball, but she responds to just plain Kitty. Somehow, the name Snowball didn't stick. She just showed up at my door one morning. Gloria found her on my doormat."

"So they get along with Toby?" Cody's curiosity got the best of him.

"Oh, yes. They play chase every morning. He just loves both of them."

"I hate to break up the conversation, but it's getting late, and we came to find out about the TNR program," Jennifer reminded them.

"Oh, sorry. I sometimes get carried away talking about my cats. Let me fill you in on what needs to be done," Miss Betty said.

She described the entire process to them, telling them the best places to look for colonies of strays, how to set up the traps, and how to care for the cats once they were in the cage.

"I never realized it was so involved," Jennifer told her. "So we have to cover the cage before we capture the cat?"

"Yes, it helps them to feel more secure and keeps them from trying to get out. The main thing is to get them to the vet as fast as possible so they don't get dehydrated. Plus, make careful note of where you captured them so you can release them in the same vicinity," Miss Betty explained.

"I'm all in. I love cats," Jennifer assured her.

"I guess I'm in, too," said Cody.

"Why don't you two go out to my garage and look over the traps I've collected? I don't drive anymore, so I use the garage as my storage area," Miss Betty told them. "My remote control for the garage door is over there on the table under that mirror."

"I see it," said Cody. "Let's go, Jennifer. We can pick out a few traps and put them in my truck."

"Okay. Just let me grab my shawl and my purse," Jennifer responded as she rose to leave. "We'll be in touch, Miss Betty. I can't wait to get started!"

"Goodbye, Miss Betty," Cody added as he picked up the remote. "I'll bring this back in and we'll be on our way in a few minutes."

Miss Betty watched as the couple headed out the door. Cody stood a head taller than Jennifer, but they still made a handsome couple. She stroked Toby's fur as she whispered in his ear, "Looks like our plan is working."

—⁓⁕⁓—

Jennifer and Cody had looked over the traps and selected four that they thought would work. They also found some large towels to drape over the traps. Jennifer decided to take the towels home and wash them.

"We'd better take these bungee cords, too. Miss Betty said that we need them to fasten the covers over the cages," Jennifer told Cody.

"They look pretty old. Maybe I'd better pick up a few new ones," he noted.

"Okay, fine by me. Just be sure to get the right size," Jennifer advised.

"Will do. I'm pretty good at measuring things, but I'll take along a few of these to go by."

Cody couldn't help but admire her as she had moved about, examining the traps and other paraphernalia that Miss Betty had collected over the years. She might be on the quiet side, but that yellow sundress made her look just like a sunflower in full bloom. She smiled a lot more than he had ever seen her smile. She was always so solemn in church except when she was singing. *Working with her wasn't going to be so bad, after all.*

Jennifer had stolen some glances of her own, watching Cody as he moved the traps around, trying to find just the right ones. He had certainly grown into a handsome man, just like his father. She could tell that he worked out by the way his muscles bulged underneath his tee-shirt. No wonder she couldn't get him out of her mind!

They headed out the garage door with Cody carrying the traps to put in his truck and Jennifer carrying the towels. Jennifer shivered as the cool night air hit her bare shoulders just as Cody let the garage door back down.

"Cold?" Cody asked her. "Here, let me help you with your shawl." He put the traps down and took the shawl Jennifer handed to him. He gently placed it around her shoulders, smoothing it down along her arms. He could feel a slight tingle running up his arms in the process.

"All better now?" he inquired.

"Much better," Jennifer replied. She was feeling a little warmer than she should. "We'd better get those traps in your truck and head home," she told him. There, she had broken the spell that was coming over her.

"You're right," he said as he picked up the traps. "I'll be in touch with you about scouting out some possible cat colonies."

"Good thinking. I'll be waiting for your call," Jennifer told him as she headed for her car.

Cody put the traps in his truck bed and headed back to the house to return the remote. He watched as Jennifer drove away. What had he gotten himself into now? he wondered.

Chapter 9

Several days passed before Jennifer heard from Cody again. In the meantime, she had been reading more about the TNR program and exactly what to do when trying to trap a feral cat. She was getting a little impatient, as she wanted to get started with the program.

Finally, her phone rang one night. The Caller I.D. showed that it was Cody. He had given her his number to program into her phone. She was thankful that her two housemates had gone to their meetings so she could converse alone without enduring any wisecracks from them.

"Hello," she answered.

"Hello. It's Cody. I apologize for taking so long to call you, but things have been rather hectic around the police station. There have been a lot of robberies lately. A lot of things have been missing, including pets. There are no wild dogs or coyotes in the area, and we haven't located the culprits yet."

"Pets? Why would someone want to steal a pet?" Jennifer asked.

"We have no clue, but it seems to be mostly cats. Very few dogs have been taken."

"Cats should be harder to steal, seeing how most of them live inside except for the feral cats," said Jennifer.

"Yes, but some people always think their cats need air and should be put outside every day. They don't realize how dangerous it is to put the cats out. Anything could happen to them."

"Oh, dear. I suppose we need to start an education program about that, too," Jennifer told him.

"What do you mean by 'too'? What else are you doing?"

"Well, my housemates and I have decided to have a fundraising party to raise money for the TNR program and also for fostering cats," Jennifer explained.

"Sounds like fun," he said.

"It will be. I hope you can come."

"Do you have the date set yet?" he asked.

"No, but I'll let you know when we do."

"Great, but that's not what I called to talk about. I have a free weekend. Are you ready to try trapping some cats?" he inquired.

"Anytime you are. Would Sunday evening after church work for you?"

"It would work just fine," he told her.

"By the way, I've been driving around looking for some feral colonies. I spotted a couple. I started putting out food and water for them. I'll skip the food for one colony Saturday, so they should be hungry by Sunday night," she said.

"I never thought of that. I guess I must not have been listening if Miss Betty told us about that."

"I guess you weren't," she noted. "But what about changing clothes? I can't go trapping cats in heels and a dress."

"Tell you what. Let's bring a change of clothes and we can change in the church bathrooms. We'll go in my truck and you can leave your car at the church parking lot. We'll swing back by there to get it when we're through."

"Hmm…that might work." Jennifer spoke thoughtfully. "I guess my car would be safe there."

"Sure, it will. I'll have a couple of patrol cars swing by every half hour. Plus, there's plenty of good lighting on the parking lot if it gets dark before we get back," Cody promised.

"Okay, that's what we'll do. See you at church Sunday evening."

True to his word, Cody drove to the church parking lot with the traps in the back of his truck. He spotted Jennifer's car and pulled in beside it. The car was empty, so she must have already gone inside, he reasoned.

He walked in and noticed that Jennifer wasn't sitting in her usual place. The pew she was using was empty except for her. He approached rather timidly and smiled down at her when she looked up to see him standing beside her.

"Is this seat taken?" he asked.

"Not anymore," she answered, as she scooted over to make room for him.

Oh, boy, now we'll be the talk of the church, he thought. He tried hard to concentrate on the sermon, but it wasn't easy.

Jennifer squirmed a little in her seat as the service progressed. He could sense that she, too, was a little uncomfortable with all eyes upon them.

They were both glad when the service ended. They headed out to their vehicles to get their change of clothes.

"I hope you brought something warm enough for these cool nights we've been having," he told her.

"It's not going to be cool much longer," she said. "Springtime soon becomes summertime."

"Just a light sweater would be enough," he said.

"I haven't forgotten about that night at Miss Betty's. I got a little chilled then. So, I came prepared."

"Great! Do you think we need insect repellant?"

"I don't think we should use that. The cats might smell it, and it could keep them away."

"Right again. I still have a lot to learn about trapping feral cats."

"Well, the best way to learn is to get started, so let's hurry up and change and be on our way," she advised.

Five minutes later they were sitting in Cody's truck and headed to the place where Jennifer had spotted the first colony. It was near the dumpster behind the hospital cafeteria. She had found some shrubs nearby where they could hide after they placed the traps.

"Did you bring some really smelly food?" he asked as they reached their destination.

"Did I! I got a can of sardines. If they can't smell that, they can't smell anything!" she exclaimed.

After Cody set the trap doors, Jennifer covered the bottom of the traps with newspaper. Then Cody placed them near the dumpsters but out of the way of traffic. Jennifer opened the can of sardines and dribbled some of the juice on the ground in front of the traps. She then dropped a small amount of food in trails leading to the trap doors. After that, she put a spoonful of the smelly stuff in the back of each trap.

"I think we're all set," she said. "All we have to do is watch and wait."

"Let's get behind the shrubs fast before some of the cats spot us," he said.

They made their way back behind the shrubs and crouched down and waited to see if their trick would work. It didn't take long for some cats to appear. It was a little past dusk, and the moon was just coming out.

"There comes one now," Jennifer whispered.

A gray striped tabby appeared, followed by two calico cats. They nosed around the traps suspiciously but didn't go in.

"Well, at least we know the calico cats are female," Jennifer noted. They have more than two colors.

"What about the gray one?" Cody asked.

"I can't tell from here, but judging by the size, I think it's a male. He must be the pack leader. I wish we were a little closer so we could see them better."

"Three cats. That's all it takes to make a colony?" he half-whispered.

"There are more than three. They didn't all come tonight. Maybe the others found some food somewhere else. They also eat bugs and rats, you know."

"I see," said Cody, still speaking softly. "But if none of them are going into the traps, we're wasting our time."

"Patience, my boy. Patience. That's the main thing that helps you to trap cats. Sometimes you could be out for hours and not trap even one cat."

"Now you tell me!" He acted a little annoyed, but he wasn't annoyed at all when he got to spend time with Jennifer. She looked prettier than ever in the moonlight, which was growing brighter by the minute.

"Hold on. I think something is about to happen," she whispered excitedly.

The gray tabby was circling the trap, stopping to smell the food every time he passed the trap. He stopped at the trap door and stuck his head in. Then he backed up and looked around. The two calico cats were watching his every move.

He stuck his head in a little further and then decided to go in all the way. As he walked gingerly towards the spoonful of sardines, he triggered the mechanism that shut the trap door. Realizing he was caught, he immediately began to turn round and round, hitting the sides of the trap and yowling loudly. The two calico cats ran away as the noise continued.

"We've got him!" Cody said excitedly.

"Oh, no," Jennifer lamented.

"What's wrong? I thought you wanted to trap a cat."

"I did, but we didn't fasten the towel tight enough. It's starting to come loose."

"No problem. I have a fire blanket in my truck. It's a habit I formed when responding to car fires," he explained as she looked at him as if he had suddenly grown a second head.

"Well, hurry up and get it before the cat hurts himself," Jennifer instructed.

Cody hurried to his truck, removed the blanket, and wrapped it around the trap. The yowling immediately ceased, and the cat stopped thrashing about. Cody picked up the trap and carried it back to his truck.

"He's riding in the back," Cody informed Jennifer. "I'm not having the smelly sardines in my new truck."

"I guess he'll be warm enough wrapped in the blanket. Do you have anything to tie it down with?" she asked.

"As a matter of fact, I also have some rope in the truck. I've learned to be prepared for just about anything since I became a police officer." He was pulling the rope out as he spoke. He tied it securely around the blanket and carefully placed the trap and the cat in the truck bed.

"I don't think the rest of the cats are coming back tonight," Jennifer said.

"I guess you're right. Let me get those other traps, and we'll call it a night."

Cody retrieved the traps and put them in the back of his truck. Then he climbed into the cab where Jennifer was waiting.

"Let's get him back to my house," Jennifer told him.

"We have to get your car first," he reminded her, as she seemed to have forgotten about it in the excitement.

"Right. We'll swing by the church and pick it up. Then it's on to my place."

"I know the way. It's right by my parents' house."

"Of course. I had almost forgotten who owned the house," she said.

They made it back to the church, and Jennifer headed for her car. Cody waited until she had started it and drove down the road. He followed her closely, so they arrived at her house together.

"Where do you want to put him?" Cody asked as he got out of the truck and picked up the trap gently.

"I guess we'll have to put him in the utility room," she decided. "Maybe we can take your blanket off and put my towel on before you leave."

"Great idea. I don't think the blanket will ever be the same. I'll think of sardines every time I look at it now."

"You can have it cleaned," she reminded him.

"Thanks a lot. Get the towel, and we'll do the switch out here. No use of scaring your housemates with all the yowling again."

He loosened the rope and slowly removed the blanket. The cat was sitting crouched in one corner of the cage, but he remained quiet. He still looked pretty upset. Jennifer draped her towel around the cage, and Cody fastened the bungee cords around it and picked it up to take it into the house.

"Lead the way," he instructed.

Jennifer unlocked the front door and held it open as Cody entered. Her two friends were sitting in the living room again, watching TV.

"Hi, girls," she greeted them. "We have our first TNR cat. This is my partner in crime, Cody Hawthorne." She motioned him towards the kitchen, which was next to the utility room.

Cody nodded at the women as he made his way through the living room and headed in the direction Jennifer was going. She turned on the lights ahead of him.

"Here we are. Just set him down right here. I'll get him to the vet the first thing in the morning. I just wish there was some way to get the sardines out of the trap."

"I have a feeling that food might be gone in the morning," he told her. "You said the cats hadn't eaten in two days. Give him a little time to settle down in a dark room, and he'll probably eat it and go to sleep."

"I hope so. I have a night light in here. Let me turn it on."

They walked back into the living room where the other two housemates were still huddled on the couch, all giggles and smiles.

"So, this is Cody," Donna commented. "We've heard about you."

"All good, I hope."

"Oh, sure," Laura said.

"Well, nice meeting both of you, but I have to run. I have an eight o'clock shift in the morning."

Jennifer walked him to the door. "Thanks for your help, Cody. I couldn't have done it without you. I hope your blanket comes clean."

"Goodnight. We'll try it again soon," he promised.

Jennifer turned back to face her housemates after closing the door.

"There was a blanket involved?" Donna asked incredulously.

"Yes, tell us more," Laura insisted.

"Oh, it was nothing. The towel we were using to cover the cage came loose, so we had to use his fire blanket he had in his truck. I fear it now smells like sardines."

They all began to laugh as Jennifer went on to describe the entire incident to them.

"Well, at least you trapped your first cat," said Donna.

"Yes, that's the good thing," Jennifer replied.

"No, the good thing is you spent almost half the night with Cody Hawthorne," Laura reminded her.

"Say what you will. It was a business deal," Jennifer declared.

"Yeah, sure. If you say so," Donna replied as she and Laura both snickered.

"I'm going to bed. Catching cats is a tiring and dirty business," Jennifer told them as she headed up the stairs. "I have to get the cat to the vet in the morning."

"Okay. Goodnight. We'll be up as soon as we finish watching this movie," said Donna.

Jennifer headed towards her room, glad that the experience was over and doubly glad it had been with Cody. She wondered if God had a hand in it. She had a lot to think about now.

Chapter 10

The following morning Jennifer was up earlier than usual. She had to drop the cat by the vet's office before she headed to work. She had sent a text to the office last night letting them know that she would be bringing in a TNR cat.

Some of the staff members were waiting for her when she arrived, and one of the young male assistants came to her car to retrieve the cat trap, still covered with the towel. She had set it on a plastic sheet, as some of her research had suggested.

"Wow, this cat is heavy. It must be a male," he stated.

"Yes, a gray striped tabby. He's a fighter, too," Jennifer told him.

She followed the assistant into one of the examination rooms where the vet was waiting for them. It was Ramona Pitkin, one of her school mates.

"Hi, Jennifer," she said. "Let's see what we have here. Did you have much trouble trapping him?"

"Not too much," Jennifer replied. "However, we were pretty far away when he got into the trap, and after that, it was chaos until we got him covered with a blanket."

"I see you replaced the blanket with a towel," Ramona commented as she loosened the bungee cords and began to remove the covering. Then she started laughing.

"What's wrong?" Jennifer asked.

"You forgot to check for the ear tipping. This cat has already been caught."

By then, the assistant had joined Ramona in laughing.

"Oh, no! How am I ever going to break the news to Cody. He will be so put out with me!" Jennifer lamented.

"Are you talking about Cody Hawthorne?" asked Ramona.

"The one and only," Jennifer replied. "How do you know who he is?"

"Oh, just about everybody in Summerfield knows Cody. After all, his dad is now the police chief, and he looks just like his dad. Well, it's not the first time somebody made the same mistake. Those tips are pretty small. Why don't you get a set of binoculars so you can see the cats better next time?"

"Great idea! I'm pretty sure Cody has a pair of binoculars, being a police officer. I'll ask if we can use those."

"No problem. Let me check the record on this guy." She flipped through a file as she spoke. "Yes, here it is. He was brought in last year. I'll give him a rabies shot for good measure. We'll keep him in the cage here with some food and water and you can pick him up after work and return him to his territory."

"Okay." Jennifer let out a sigh as she spoke. "I guess I'll have to break the news to Cody."

"See you later today," Ramona said as Jennifer turned to leave.

Jennifer pulled her phone out of her purse after she sat down in her car. She supposed that Cody would already be at work now, as it was almost 8 a.m. She thought the better of it, as she was about to be late herself. She would call him after she got to the fire station.

She drove through the traffic, almost in a daze. How could she have been so dumb? It was like she had forgotten most of what Miss Betty had told her to do. She had been running on adrenaline, and being so close to Cody during that time hadn't helped any. It had her adrenaline pumped up even more. He *was* good-looking, and she hadn't been on a real date in quite some time. There just hadn't been anybody she was interested in. Not until she was paired up with Cody. She wondered if Cody felt the same way.

After she got to the fire station, she hurried to punch into the time clock. She made it just as the clock hands hit 8 a.m. She changed into her firefighter's pants and tee-shirt. Relieved that she would not be chastised for arriving late, she walked into the lounge area, where several of her fellow firefighters were watching TV. A few of the night staff had just finished eating breakfast and were about to leave. Several of her team greeted her while others just waved, as they were absorbed in their TV show.

"So, how did your cat trapping work out?" asked Freddie.

"Oh, we caught the cat," Jennifer replied.

"Just one?" Freddie seemed extra curious.

"The others ran away before we could get them. Hopefully, we'll have better luck next time," Jennifer explained.

"Okay. I just hope you don't make that your second career. We can't afford to lose our first female firefighter," Don told her.

"Oh, no chance of that. I couldn't let all of my training go to waste," she assured him. "Excuse me, guys, but I need to make a phone call," she said as she headed towards the bunk area.

As soon as she was sure she was out of earshot, she pulled up Cody's cell phone number and punched it in. She waited as she heard it ring several times. To her relief, he picked up after the third ring.

"Hello, Jennifer," he said, as her name and number had shown up on his Caller I.D.

"Cody, I'm afraid I've got some bad news for you. We should have been more observant. Turns out that the cat we caught has already been caught and released once, so we really didn't do much for the cat population."

"Oh, no. I can't believe it! Seems like he would have been smarter than to get caught again."

"I guess he was hungry, and those sardines were really tempting," Jennifer joked.

"I guess so. What do we do now?"

"Well, the vet is holding him in the cage for us until I get off work. Do you think we could haul him back in your truck? I really hate to have that cage in the back seat of my car."

"Sure, I can help you out. What time do I need to be there?"

"The vet's office closes at 6 p.m. I can go ahead and get the cage if you can't make it by then. I'll wait outside for you."

"Okay, give me the address, and I'll be there."

Jennifer proceeded to give him the directions. She was relieved that she wouldn't have to handle the cage all by herself. She began to formulate a plan for another attempt to catch some more cats at a different location.

Cody showed up a little past 5:30 p.m. to find Jennifer standing beside her car with the cage on the ground next to her. She had changed out of her firefighter's uniform and had her hair tied back into a ponytail. It set off her face, which sported the strong, square jaw of her mother, Luci Carlito Clark. She looked as if she could tackle the world. He wondered if she ever wished she had a man to help her do that.

"I see you have that cat waiting for me," he commented as he exited his truck.

"Yes, we're both ready for this experience to be over," she said, her brown eyes flashing as she spoke.

Cody picked up the trap and headed towards his truck. He noticed that the paper in the bottom was wet.

"Oh, looks like somebody had to 'go,'" he noted.

"Yes, they gave him some water to keep him hydrated. I wish I could have taken him back this morning, but I had to go to work. Let's hurry before he has to stay in that cage any longer."

They both peered inside the front of the cage after Cody set it in the truck bed. The cat was still crouched in the back, looking unhappy.

"Well, at least he's not trying to tear his way out of the cage now," Jennifer said. "Let's get going!"

They both climbed into their vehicles and headed towards the back of the hospital cafeteria. When they arrived, they were relieved to see that the parking lot there was almost empty.

Cody removed the cage from his truck and carried it back to the place where they had captured the cat. He put on some heavy gloves, as Miss Betty had recommended, before releasing the trap door.

The cat sprang out the door and paused briefly before taking off at a fast trot to the space behind the dumpster. He didn't even look back.

"Well, so much for that tabby," Jennifer commented. "I have another place we can try later in the week. If you're willing, that is."

"Yes, I'm willing, provided it fits into my schedule. What evening did you have in mind?

"How about Thursday evening?" she asked.

"That's fine with me if I don't get extra duty. There have been some reports of more cat nabbings around town. Sergeant Phillips is all worked up about it. His wife's cat was one of those who has gone missing, and she's about to drive him nuts. If he doesn't find the cat soon, he might be sleeping on the couch."

"If I recall, he's no small person," Jennifer commented.

"No, nobody tangles with Sergeant Phillips," Cody told her.

They both laughed, picturing the scene of the blustery sergeant trying to fit his heavy frame on a couch as a bed. He never gave Cody a hard time, considering that his dad was the police chief, but plenty of other young policemen had been dressed down as the sergeant's temper flared.

"Okay, then. I'll skip feeding those cats on Wednesday, and we'll try that spot Thursday," Jennifer decided.

"Why don't I just swing by your house and pick you up next time? No use in riding in two vehicles."

"You're right. Let's meet about 6:30 p.m. or so. It'll be getting dark by 8 p.m. I know just the spot to put the traps."

"Sure thing. I'll clean up this one." He looked at the wet paper in disgust. "Then I'll bring the others with me, too."

"Thank you so much for keeping them for me. Those housemates of mine are so picky. They would be complaining about 'smelly cat traps' if I kept them."

"Well, I live alone, so no problem there."

"I'll see you Thursday evening, then," she said as she prepared to get into her car.

Cody quickly loaded the trap into his truck bed and headed back to his apartment. However, catching cats was the last thing on his mind. Jennifer now occupied his thoughts most of the time when he wasn't working. He had avoided women almost as much as his dad had before he met Cody's mom, Holly, now deceased. He wondered how he let himself get so involved with a woman.

Chapter 11

Two weeks had passed since Jonas had trimmed Miss Betty's shrubs. It was time for him to tend Miss Betty's garden again. He showed up on Saturday morning with his two great-nephews accompanying him. He rang Miss Betty's doorbell when he arrived to let her know that he would be having some helpers.

Miss Betty was surprised to see two school-aged boys dressed in work clothes standing with Jonas on her front porch. She had not met them before.

"Miss Betty, these are my two great-nephews, Sam and John, Adolphus's boys. They're goin' to be workin' with me today in your garden if that's okay with you. I'm tryin' to teach them a little about gardening so they can earn some extra money for school."

"Why, Jonas, what a wonderful idea. Just be sure they don't do anything to harm my roses," Miss Betty warned him.

"Oh, don't you worry, Miss Betty. I know those roses are your pride and joy. Nobody but Jonas touches them," he assured her, tapping his chest as he spoke.

"So, are you boys planning to be gardeners, too, like your Uncle Jonas and your dad?" she asked.

"Oh, no, Miss Betty. I know how hard it is for a black man with no education. These two boys are good students, and they plan on goin' to college, don't you, boys?"

"Yes, Uncle Jonas," Sam replied. "I want to be a dentist, and John wants to get into R.O.T.C. and go into the military."

"Both fine careers," Miss Betty noted. "I'm so happy you're making good decisions."

"Yes, Adolphus and I started trainin' them early to want to be good students and to make good grades," said Jonas. "Well, you look after those cats, Miss Betty, and we'll look after your garden."

"Oh, I will, Jonas, and I know you'll do a good job. I'll come out later before you leave and admire your handiwork."

Jonas and the boys headed for the garden, and Miss Betty went back inside to read her paper. She had already eaten breakfast. She was waiting for a report on how the first cat trapping had gone with Cody and Jennifer.

The phone rang a little after 8 a.m. Miss Betty answered and was relieved to hear Jennifer's voice on the other end of the line. She had begun to worry about the project and wondered if she had made the right decision in pairing Jennifer and Cody.

"Jennifer, it's so good to hear from you. Why did it take you so long to call, and how did the cat trapping go?" She asked.

"It was an adventure," Jennifer admitted. "I was hoping to trap more cats than we did on our first try. That's why I haven't called you sooner. We had three cats in our sights, but we got just one of them. Then, after I got him to the vet's, it turned out he was ear-tipped, so he had already been neutered."

"Oh, no." Miss Betty could hardly believe it. "How could you have missed that?"

"Well, it was getting dark by then. By the time he decided to go in the cage, as soon as the trap door fell, he just went wild. He was jumping around and yowling so loud that it scared the other cats away. I couldn't get a good look at him before we covered him up."

"I see," said Miss Betty. "Try using some binoculars next time."

"Yes, that's what the vet suggested, and Cody has a pair we can use."

"I hope the vet wasn't too upset about the mix-up."

"No, she checked the records and gave him a rabies booster. I had to wait until I got off work before Cody and I returned him to his territory. We're using Cody's truck to transport them so the interior of my car won't get messed up."

"Sounds like a good idea. Are you and Cody getting along?" Miss Betty inquired cautiously, not wanting to seem too pushy.

"Yes, so far everything is working out fine between us. Cody wasn't too mad about the mix-up. He was a pretty good sport about it. We're going out again next Thursday to a different spot. By the way, have you heard that cats have been disappearing around town?"

"Yes, Gloria told me. I don't get out much, you know. I keep all the cats inside now."

"Right. I haven't been back to get Toby out of that tree," Jennifer said.

"He's a total housecat now. He's content to stay inside with the other cats."

"That's good to know. Just be careful and don't let any of them out with these cat nabbers around."

"Oh, I won't. I certainly won't," Miss Betty assured her.

She settled down to read her newspaper after talking to Jennifer. Gloria was coming just once a day now since the dogs were gone. She washed the breakfast dishes and fixed Miss Betty's lunch and changed the litter boxes when necessary. She still kept up her schedule of cooking on Mondays, so there was someone to check on Miss Betty every day.

The doorbell rang after a couple of hours. It was Jonas, asking Miss Betty to come out and inspect the work that he and his great-nephews had done. Miss Betty picked up her cane and walked into the garden, deeply inhaling the scent of the spring flowers. She looked around, appreciating the array of colors surrounding her.

"I mowed the grass, and the boys did the weed eatin' and blew off the cobblestones for me," Jonas told her.

"Well, they certainly did a fine job," Miss Betty said. "You boys are going to be just as good with plants as your dad and your Uncle Jonas."

"We hope so, Miss Betty, but we're saving our money for college," Sam informed her.

"Yes, we know we don't make a lot of money, but we have a long time to work for it," John added.

"You are two mighty smart young men. I think you're definitely headed in the right direction," said Miss Betty. "Are you going to try to get some more yard work?"

"Yes, I'm goin' to get them a small self-propelled lawn mower so they can mow some small yards," Jonas told her.

"That's right. We're too young to drive, so we can't operate the riding mowers," Sam added.

"I wish you the best, and you come back any time and help Jonas when you're not in school," Miss Betty told them.

"I'm goin' to pay them part of my salary when they help me," said Jonas.

Grins spread across their faces as they heard that remark. It was just the incentive they needed.

"You boys be careful, and you, too, Jonas. I've just heard that there are some cat nabbers in town. You don't want to run into any of them."

"You're so right, Miss Betty. I'll make sure they're safe," Jonas assured her as he walked her back to her front door.

"Now you keep all your doors and windows locked, Miss Betty," he warned.

"I will, Jonas. Thank you so much for doing your usual excellent job, and thank you, too, Sam and John."

"Goodbye, Miss Betty," they responded in unison as they headed for Jonas' truck.

"Can we ride in the back, Uncle Jonas?" John asked.

"Now, boys, you know I tol' you and tol' you that it's not safe to ride back there. Besides, it's against the law."

"Oh, okay. We'll sit in the cab," John agreed reluctantly.

Jonas drove off after all three of them were inside the truck, and the boys waved at Miss Betty, who was still standing in her doorway. She slowly closed the door and locked it.

I can't believe we have cat nabbers in town. I just hope none of my babies disappear, she thought as she headed back to her recliner, feeling in the mood for her morning nap.

Chapter 12

Cody showed up at Jennifer's house promptly at 6:30 Thursday evening, as they had discussed. Jennifer was waiting at the door and walked out when she saw his truck pull up to the curb. Both of her housemates had gone to their respective classes, so at least she wouldn't have to endure their inquiries about her "date" with Cody again. Some "date." If only they knew how hard it was to catch a feral cat. She hoped she and Cody would have better luck this time.

Cody got out of his truck and opened the passenger door for Jennifer. She wasted no time climbing into the roomy cab. She clutched two cans of sardines and a spoon, along with some old newspapers. Cody had brought everything else they needed.

"Thanks for picking me up, Cody," she said. "By the way, you certainly have a nice truck. It looks brand new."

"It is," Cody replied. "I was driving the same one I had in high school, and it was about worn out. I don't really have a lot of expenses, so I splurged on this truck."

I love the color," said Jennifer. "I think silver trucks are always so neat."

"Thanks," Cody told her. "It's one of my favorite colors for a vehicle, too."

"We're heading for a new destination. Let's try the area around the children's playground. There are some trees and other places outside the fence where we can hide and watch the traps."

"Do you really think cats would be hanging around a playground with so much activity?" Cody asked.

"Where there are children, there's food. I spotted what looked like a few stray cats when I was scouting around earlier this week. I went back and put out some food."

"Okay, if you say so, but I can't see cats hanging around such a noisy, busy place."

"Trust me. I believe they will come out when it's almost dark," Jennifer told him.

It didn't take very long to reach the playground. Cody parked the truck on the opposite side of where Jennifer indicated she wanted to set up the traps. He began to gather the traps. Cody had already secured the towels around the traps with the bungee cords. Jennifer picked up her two cans of sardines, the spoon, and the newspapers and set them inside one of the traps for transport.

They walked to a secluded place alongside the playground, each carrying two traps. Jennifer indicated where the traps should be placed. After Cody had arranged them and set the traps, she put the newspapers in the bottom and then began her ritual of distributing the zigzag streams of juice and small bits of food leading up to the trap openings. Cody took the spoon and placed a spoonful of sardines in the back of each trap.

"Thanks for your help. It was a little hard for me to reach that far back," she told him.

"Yes, I noticed that the last time. Well, let's get ourselves out of sight and see what happens," he said.

They moved cautiously away from the traps and found a good hiding place behind a large tree.

"Did you bring your binoculars?" Jennifer asked as an afterthought.

"Yes, I have them here around my neck. Didn't you notice?"

"No, I was so busy concentrating on getting the traps ready that I forgot all about them," she confessed.

Cody smiled. "Good thing you've got a partner, partner."

"You're so right, partner." The corners of her mouth turned up as she spoke, and Cody was again amazed at how her eyes lit up every time she smiled.

They stopped talking and began to watch the traps. Cody had a large wristwatch, so it was easy for him to keep up with how long they had been there. It wasn't long before several cats appeared, moving slowly along the fence of the playground. They stopped often and looked around as if they thought somebody might be watching them.

Jennifer touched her finger to her lips as a sign to Cody to be totally silent. It was then that he noticed how perfectly formed her lips were. He wondered what it would be like to kiss them. He shook his head slightly, willing himself to keep his mind on the cats.

Jennifer motioned to him to use his binoculars and pointed to her ears as a signal to check for ear tipping. He understood immediately. He didn't want a repeat of their last experience. He raised the binoculars and began a scan of the three cats who were marching down the fence row.

He mouthed, "It's okay" to Jennifer, assuring her that none of the cats had tipped ears. She smiled and nodded. It looked as if they might be having better luck this time, if only the cats took the bait.

The bravest of the three moved towards one of the traps, raising its head to sniff the air as the smell of sardines was undoubtedly attracting it.

It moved closer and took a nibble of a tidbit of food Jennifer had lined up in front of the trap, along with some inside. Pausing to look around, the cat entered the trap and headed towards the back, tripping the trap door. It jumped briefly as the door shut but kept heading towards the food.

Jennifer put her hand over her mouth to keep from laughing. Cody was smiling, too. It looked like they might have at least one victory. If only the cat kept quiet.

The other two cats were intent on following the food trails at the other traps. They had jumped slightly as the first trap door shut, but the temptation of the food was too great. They were really hungry! Both of them continued to follow the food trail until they tripped the trap doors on two of the other traps.

"We've got three!" Jennifer whispered excitedly.

Cody gave a fist pump in the air.

They waited a while longer. The cats were beginning to pace in the cages, as they had eaten all the food. It looked like three was going to be their limit for the night.

Jennifer stood up. "I think that's all we're going to catch tonight," she said.

"I think you're right," Cody agreed. "Let's get the ones we caught and be on our way. I'm going to get my truck and move it closer so we don't have to carry the traps so far."

"Good idea," Jennifer told him. "I'll wait beside the cages."

Cody made short work of driving up and retrieving the cat traps, carefully loading them into the bed of his truck. All the cats had grown anxious and were huddled in the back of the cages. Jennifer lowered the towels to cover more of each cage, trying to make the cats feel more secure.

"Poor babies. I feel sorry having to keep them caged all night, but it's for their own good."

"They'll never know it," Cody observed.

"No, but I will," said Jennifer.

"I hope your housemates won't get too upset with three cats in the house."

"They're out for a while. I hope they'll still be gone when we get back. How long have we been here?" she asked.

Cody looked at his watch. "It's a little after 8 p.m.," he told her.

"Hmm…not as long as it seemed," she commented.

"It didn't seem long at all to me," Cody said.

Jennifer looked up to meet his eyes. His brilliant blue eyes that still showed up in the moonlight that was now out.

"Maybe you're right," she admitted. "Let's get moving and beat my housemates back to the house!"

Cody opened the passenger door again for her, and she climbed into the cab, feeling a little more comfortable this time. She could get used to riding in such a large vehicle instead of her smaller car, she decided.

He walked around, climbed in, and started the truck. He set the truck in gear and headed back to Jennifer's house.

She was relieved to see that no other cars were there yet. Hopefully, they could get the cats into the utility room before anybody else got home.

Cody carried the traps in one at a time after Jennifer unlocked the door. She turned on the night light and shut the door to the utility room. The cats were safe for the night.

"I don't know how I'll get all of them to the vet's tomorrow morning." She looked worried as she spoke.

"Why don't I run by here and pick them up for you?" Cody asked.

"Would you?"

"Of course. I wouldn't offer if I didn't plan to actually do it. I always keep my promises."

"You know, somehow, I believe you do," she told him.

Cody cleared his throat. His face turned slightly red. Then he spoke. "How would you like to go to the movies with me this weekend?"

"The movies? I love movies. Of course, I'll go with you," she said.

He grinned. "What do you want to see?"

"What do you want to see?"

"Is there an echo in here?" he teased.

"Oh, I don't know. Just try to find one without too much violence or bad language," she said.

"Yes, I don't think our preacher would approve of most of those they show today. I'll check the schedule and let you know what time to be ready," he told her as he prepared to leave.

"It's a date," she said, smiling up at him again.

He walked back to his truck, and she closed the door behind him. Both of them had a lot to think about before Saturday night.

Chapter 13

Jennifer's housemates arrived home shortly after Cody left. They came through the door still excited about their respective lessons, chattering away as they entered the living room. Jennifer had already been upstairs and showered and changed clothes. She was sitting in the living room watching TV.

"Hey, girlfriend, how was the cat trapping tonight?" Donna asked.

"It was pretty successful. We got three cats this time," Jennifer informed her.

"Oh, where are they? Did you put them in the utility room again?" Laura asked.

"Yes, they're there with just the night light on. It's best not to disturb them," Jennifer cautioned.

"Oh, shoot. I was hoping to get a peek at them. What do they look like?" Laura continued questioning her.

"I think they're all females. They were pretty calm, unlike that gray tabby who just about tore the cage apart. They're just crouched in the back of the cages as far as they can get," Jennifer explained.

"How are you going to get three cages in that car of yours tomorrow? Don't you need to get them to the vet right away?" Donna asked.

"Yes, I already texted her that they'll arrive tomorrow morning about 7:30," Jennifer responded.

"So, you still didn't answer the question about how you plan to fit three cages into your car." Donna prodded her for an explanation.

"That's all taken care of. Cody has agreed to pick them up in his truck."

"Cody again, huh? You two seem to be getting pretty close," Laura noted. "Is there a hint of romance in the air?"

Jennifer blushed before she answered. "I can't say for sure, but I think I might be feeling something for him. I don't know if he feels the same about me. He asked me to go to the movies with him on Saturday."

"The movies--that's a start. Definitely better than hanging out in the bushes waiting for cats to show up," Donna told her.

"I guess you're right," Jennifer agreed. "We'll just to see what happens. Only God knows the answer to that right now."

"God always knows. Just trust in Him. I know you're a faithful church goer," said Laura.

"Yes, my mom and dad always made sure Brian and I went to church. They believed that God brought them together the first time and again after they split up. They have a really good marriage now, one like I hope I can have."

"You hang in there, girl. Your dreams will come true soon. I just feel it," said Donna.

"I hope so. Now my biggest problem is figuring out what to wear Saturday night."

"Well, before that, we have a report to make to you about the fundraising party," Laura announced. "We found a place, and they agreed to let us use it for free as long as we make sure it's left clean afterwards."

"Where would that be?" Jennifer asked.

"The City Convention Center, of course. Plus, I found a band. They're good, but just starting out, so they're willing to provide the music free."

"That's great!" Jennifer exclaimed. "But what about the food?"

"Have your forgotten about Rosalena's, your dad's restaurant?" Donna asked.

"Why didn't I think of that? I've been so preoccupied with the cats and my job that it just didn't enter my mind. You see, my parents turned the running of the restaurant over to James Lovett years ago. He's their most trusted employee. We still go there for a family meal every once in a while, especially when Brian comes to town to visit. Mama Rosa and Papa D'Armon are getting up in age now. Papa sold his taxi cab business to my Uncle Anthony, so they mostly just stay at home. Mama Rosa still cooks her Italian dishes, but it doesn't take as much food for just her and Papa D'Armon. She always keeps some sugar cookies on hand in case I pop in for a visit," Jennifer told them.

"Your family does have the best restaurant in town," Laura said. "I've been there several times."

"So, do you think you could get them to supply the food for our party?" Donna asked.

"I'm sure I can. I'll talk to James about it. He's so creative. I know he can come up with something delicious and easy to eat," Jennifer replied. "Let me get these cats taken care of tomorrow, and I'll get right on it."

"We picked a date, too," Laura told her. "It's May Day. We thought that would be a good time to celebrate spring and help the cat project at the same time."

"Oh, what fun," Jennifer said. "Maybe we can have a Maypole dance for the children."

"I think they would love that," said Donna. "In the meantime, we'll think of some more fun activities for the adults."

"I've done enough thinking for tonight. I have to get up early and get the cats to the vet's," Jennifer reminded them.

"Yes, it's about time to head to bed," Laura agreed. "No romantic movies tonight."

"Jennifer can just dream about her own romance," Donna commented jokingly.

"Yes," Laura sighed. "I just hope some of those good-looking firefighters or police officers show up at our fundraising event."

The trio headed upstairs, each with something different on their minds. They were all hoping for happy dreams.

Chapter 14

Jennifer was up early again the next morning. She ate a hasty breakfast and did a quick check on the cats. They were still quiet and sitting in the back of their cages.

"Don't worry. You're about to go for another ride," she told them, as if they knew what she was talking about. She hoped Cody would show up soon.

She had no sooner put her breakfast dishes in the sink than the doorbell rang. She hurried to answer it, and it was Cody, as he had promised.

"Well, here I am," he announced unnecessarily. "Are the cats ready to go?"

"They can't talk, but I think they are. I'm sure they're tired of staying in those strange cages," Jennifer replied.

"Here's hoping there's no wet newspaper this time," he noted.

"I haven't given them any water since they're having surgery. Turns out they're all females this time. I know that much from their coloring."

They walked into the utility room, and Cody began to carry the cages to his truck, insisting that he should do it instead of Jennifer.

"You follow me in your car, and then we can both head straight for work," he said.

"I'm with you on that one. I was almost late the last time," she told him.

With the three cages loaded and secured, they headed for the vet's office. They dropped off the cats with a promise to pick them up later in the day, provided no complications arose during the surgeries.

Both of them managed to get to work on time. Jennifer's arrival was uneventful, but Cody's was livelier. He sat in on a session about the cat nabbers. It seemed that they were growing bolder, and more and more cats were disappearing. Sergeant Phillips' wife's cat was still among those missing, so he was on a tear.

"I don't care how we do it, but we have to start searching every empty building and warehouse in the city. Those cats have to be here somewhere," he told his crew. "Keep your eyes and ears open at all times when you're out on patrol."

Cody was paired up with another policeman named George Fairly because the sergeant wanted two men together at all times. They didn't know who the cat nabbers were or if they were armed and dangerous. After they left the meeting, Cody drove while his partner scanned the area as they went up and down the streets methodically. They didn't see anything unusual. Then Cody spotted it. There was an unmarked white van in one of the neighborhoods. They drove up behind it after calling it in. They got out of their patrol car and approached the van cautiously. They saw one man sitting behind the wheel.

"Come out of the van with your hands up," Cody instructed as they neared the van with their weapons drawn.

"What's the problem, officers?" the man asked. "I'm just waiting on my partner. We work for a plumbing company, and he's here checking on a leak."

"Plumber, huh? Let me see your driver's license," Cody instructed. "Take it out of your wallet."

"Sure, sure. No problem," the suspect replied as he removed the item from his wallet.

Cody looked it over. "It says here you live in another state. What are you doing here?"

"Oh, I just moved here. I haven't had time to get my license changed yet," the man explained.

Cody handed the license to George. "Call this in, and call in the van's license number, too," he instructed his partner.

George headed back to the cruiser to follow instructions. He came back shortly afterwards with a report.

"Turns out the driver's license is valid. So is the van's license," he told Cody.

"Still seems suspicious to me," Cody replied as another man dressed in a plumber's suit appeared from the back of the house, toolbox in hand.

"What's going on?" the man inquired.

"Just doing a little checking," Cody replied. "Do you have any I.D.?"

"Yes, I have a driver's license," the man replied as he began to remove it from his wallet.

Cody checked it and then handed it to George to call in, just to be sure.

"What's this all about?" the second man asked.

"We're just making sure the neighborhood's safe," Cody said. "I've never seen this van before, and it has no markings on it. I find that a little strange for a company van."

"Oh, we're just renting this one. Ours is in the shop," the man explained.

George came back with the report of that driver's license also being valid.

"Okay, I guess you guys can go. Just be careful about using an unmarked van," Cody instructed.

He and George watched as the men got back into the van and drove away.

"It still doesn't feel right to me," Cody told George. "I don't trust those two guys."

George just shrugged his shoulders. "If the I.D.'s are good, there's not much we can do."

Cody reported the incident to Sergeant Phillips at the end of the shift. The sergeant was immediately suspicious. "Keep a close eye out for unmarked vans," he told Cody. "This might be the first clue we might have in the case."

Chapter 15

C ody met Jennifer at the vet's office after work, and they returned the three cats to their territory. It didn't take them long to disappear behind the trees and bushes.

"Well, so much for that," Jennifer said. "Maybe we can try the other location again next week."

"Maybe so," Cody agreed. "However, what interests me the most right now is our date on Saturday night. I think I've found a movie you might like."

"What is it?" Jennifer asked, her eyes sparkling in anticipation, and her mouth turned up in a half-smile.

"It's a surprise," he said. "Just trust me."

"I guess turnabout's fair play. You trusted me when it came to the cats. Now it's my turn to trust you."

"I hope you'll always trust me, Jennifer," he told her.

"I plan to," she assured him.

"Just be ready at 6:30 on Saturday night. The movie starts at 7 p.m."

The week went by fast, but not fast enough for Jennifer. She was stuck, once again, with deciding what to wear. Her two housemates offered her all kinds of advice. Her head was spinning from so many suggestions.

She threw her last dress on the bed and stood looking at the pile that had accumulated. She threw up her hands and exclaimed, "I give up! I can't make up my mind which dress to choose."

Donna came up with the solution. "What about that aqua dress? Aqua is supposed to be the universally becoming color, and it would go great with your skin."

"I think you're right," agreed Jennifer. "Plus, I have some turquoise jewelry that I can wear with it."

"So, problem solved," said Laura. "But that still leaves me and Donna with no dates for tonight."

"Just wait until our fundraising event. I'm sure you'll both soon have more dates than you can handle after that," Jennifer assured them.

"Yes, we'd better get started with those tickets and the advertisements," Donna mused. "How much should we sell them for?"

"How about $20 each for adults and $10 for children?" suggested Laura.

"Sounds good to me," said Jennifer. "With all the donations, we should come out ahead. All we need to do is convince people to come. I just hope all of these cat nabbings don't discourage them. Let's hope the police find the culprits before then."

"Well, girl, look at the time. You'd better start getting ready for your date," Donna reminded her.

"You're right," said Jennifer as she began to hang the other dresses back in her closet, leaving the aqua one hanging on the closet door. "So, shoo, and I'll hurry."

"Shoo! Who do you think you are? Miss Betty shooing Toby up the tree?" Laura couldn't resist throwing in that remark.

"Toby isn't going up the tree anymore. He stays inside now, according to Miss Betty," Jennifer said.

"Good to know. Hopefully, he won't be one of the missing cats," Laura noted.

Cody showed up promptly at 6:30 p.m., as they had agreed. Jennifer answered the door and took in the scene with him standing there wearing gray pants and a blue crew neck tee shirt. It brought out the blue even more in those mesmerizing eyes of his. She visualized her two friends in the background practically falling over themselves at the sight of him. She resisted the temptation to turn around to see if her instincts were right. She was positive she heard giggling in the background.

"Ready to go?" he asked.

"Yes, I can't wait to see what your surprise movie will be," she said as she grabbed her purse and pulled the door shut behind her.

"You look very pretty tonight," he commented as they walked towards his truck.

"Thank you," Jennifer replied as he opened the passenger door for her.

True to his word, Cody had picked out a suitable movie for them to watch. It was a romantic comedy. He knew women always loved that kind of movie, even if men weren't that crazy about them.

Jennifer seemed to be really enjoying herself, laughing as the movie progressed. He had bought a bucket of popcorn for them to share and two soft drinks to go with it. Their hands touched several times as they both reached for the popcorn at the same time.

"Sorry," he whispered as it happened for the third time.

"No problem. I guess I'm just extra hungry tonight," Jennifer whispered back.

She didn't mind if their hands touched! He was making progress. He wondered if there would be a chance to steal a kiss when he took her home.

The movie ended too soon for him. Jennifer was laughing out loud at the end. She looked at him as they rose to exit the theater. She reluctantly picked up her purse, thinking that the movie had ended too soon for her, also.

"Oh, that was a good one, Cody! I'm so glad you picked it for us to watch," she commented as they walked outside.

"I'm glad you liked it," he responded. "Would you like to drive around for a little while before I take you home. It's such a nice night."

"I'd like that very much," she said.

They walked to his truck, and he once again opened the door for her. She managed to climb in, despite the heels she was wearing. He wondered why women always thought they needed to wear heels to impress a man.

"Where would you like to go?" he asked after he had climbed into the driver's seat and started the truck.

"Oh, I don't know. How about the lake?" she suggested.

"Yes, it's always beautiful in the moonlight," he said.

"Oh, so you have experience with taking girls out to view the lake?" she asked.

"Not really. I haven't done a lot of dating. I guess I take after my dad. He avoided women like the plague until my grandfather, who was the police chief at the time, paired him up with a female recruit. It didn't take him very long to change his mind about women after that. That police recruit turned out to be his wife and my mom."

"I'm so sorry about your mom being killed in that drug bust gone wrong," she told him.

"I was too young to remember much about it. But he married Jillian, who was just like a mom to me when I was growing up."

"Yes, I remember that all the kids at school loved her as a teacher. She's so beautiful." Jillian spoke thoughtfully.

"My dad has good taste. It runs in the family." Cody winked as he spoke.

They were headed for the lake when Cody hit his brakes as he spotted a white van ahead of them in the road.

"Whoa, hold on a minute!" he exclaimed suddenly.

"What's wrong?" Jennifer asked nervously.

"Do you see that white van ahead of us? It looks like the one my partner and I came across a few days ago. Everything checked out, but I still don't trust the two guys who were driving it. They're from out of town."

"Should we follow it?" Jennifer asked.

"That's what I plan to do. I have to go slow, though, so they won't know they're being followed. Help me keep watch on them."

Jennifer leaned forward in her seat, obviously excited about being in on a police excursion. "I'll do my best," she said.

The van moved slowly, pulling over to the curb occasionally. Cody stayed a safe distance behind them, stopping when they did. Then the van suddenly sped up and headed around a corner. Cody sped up, too, but by the time he turned the corner, the van was out of sight.

"I think they spotted us," he lamented. "I'll report it to Sergeant Phillips in the morning."

"You're going to call him on a Sunday?" Jennifer asked.

"Believe me, with his wife's cat missing, he'll be glad to hear any kind of report that might lead to finding all those missing cats," Cody assured her.

"Maybe you should call him now," Jennifer suggested.

"Are you kidding? He's fast asleep now. If I wake him up, he won't be in a very good mood, even if it might have something to do with the cats. Besides, the van's gone."

"I see. Well, I guess it's too late to go out to the lake now," Jennifer said.

"I suppose you're right. I'd better get you home. After all, tomorrow is a church day. We can't have you going with circles under your eyes."

Jennifer laughed. "You have a lot to learn about women. We have all kinds of tricks to conceal those circles."

"Oh, I guess I do have a lot to learn, then," he admitted.

He had turned the truck in the opposite direction and headed for Jennifer's house. The front porch light was on.

"Looks like someone is waiting for you," he said.

"Yes, those two housemates of mine are like mother hens sometimes. You can bet that they'll have lots of questions about you."

"Good luck with that. I'm not that interesting."

"I wouldn't say that. After all, I *did* go out with you." She tilted her head as she spoke.

He walked her to the front door, and they both paused. She looked up at him, and the temptation was too much for him. He bent down and gently kissed those lips he had been admiring for several weeks. He was surprised when she put her arms around his neck and kissed him back.

"I guess that will give your friends something to talk about," he said.

"They don't have to know *everything* about our date," she responded, smiling slightly. "Goodnight now. I'll see you at church tomorrow."

"Sure thing. Save me a seat." he responded.

"I'll do that," she said as she unlocked the door and headed inside.

He walked back to his truck and saw the porch light go out. Their first *real date* was over. He hoped it wouldn't be their last.

Chapter 16

Cody and Jennifer spent the next several weeks tracking down colonies of feral cats and trapping as many of them as they could. They were growing closer as they spent more time together. Neither one of them had ever gone steady with anyone, although both had occasionally dated someone. Somehow, it had never seemed to work out for either one of them.

A few days later, they were at their latest site where Jennifer had spotted a colony of feral cats. It was near the back of Rosalena's restaurant.

"I can't believe I didn't think of this as the first place to look," she told him as they sat waiting for the cats to appear.

"Yes, considering that your family owns the establishment, it seems that it would have been the first place you would have started," he commented.

"Oh, boy. If the walls in this place could talk, there would be a lot of secrets revealed," she informed him.

"Oh? How so?" he asked.

"For starters, it's what got my mom and dad together. He bought the restaurant when it was closed, and my mom was in charge of changing it into an Italian restaurant, using my grandma's recipes. They had a big argument and almost didn't get married."

"They seem so happy now. That's hard to believe."

"There are many other stories besides that one, but I don't have time to tell you about them now. Maybe someday I will," she said.

"I'd be interested to learn more about your family," he told her.

"Right now, I'm more concerned with catching some more cats," she said. "I hope they show up tonight."

They waited longer than usual, but no cats appeared on the scene. Jennifer started to fret.

"I hope those cat nabbers haven't gotten any of them," she said nervously.

"Well, so far, they seem to be interested in mostly cats people own," he told her. "We've had reports of missing cats all over town, but we can't find out who's doing it or where the cats are being held, if they're still here in town. Chances are, they might already be gone from the area. I think it has something to do with that white van I keep spotting and then losing."

"I don't care whose cats they are. I just want it to stop. They're making a lot of families unhappy," Jennifer declared.

"You're right. People get very attached to their pets. I know my dad was nuts about his dog, Duke. It was sad when he passed away from old age. My stepmom had a white Persian cat when she and my dad got married. That cat lived to be pretty old, too. They never got any more pets. They said those were irreplaceable."

"I can understand that. I know how much Miss Betty loves her cats, especially Toby. I don't know what she would do if anything happened to him."

"Oh, I think Toby's pretty safe. She keeps all her cats inside now," Cody assured her.

"Let's just hope she keeps all her doors and windows locked. Sometimes older people forget to check things like that."

"Yes, but she does have Gloria checking on her every day, and Jonas watches over her, too."

"She's lucky to have them. I'd hate to see her have to go to a nursing home."

Cody shifted his position. His legs were about to go to sleep. "I don't think the cats are coming tonight," he said.

"I think you're right," Jennifer agreed. "Let's pick up the traps and call it a night. I'm still worried about the cats, though."

They loaded everything into the truck and were ready to head home.

"We'll check again tomorrow. Maybe they'll show up then," Cody decided.

"I never did get that moonlight ride out to the lake," Jennifer reminded him.

"Yes, we've been so busy chasing cats that we haven't had time for that. I think tonight would be the perfect time. It's clear, the moon is out, and just look at those stars," he observed.

"They would look even better over the lake," Jennifer suggested.

Cody started the truck and headed in the direction of the lake. This time, he didn't plan on letting anything keep him from reaching their destination. He just hoped there wouldn't be any other couples up there taking advantage of the scenery, among other things.

As he pulled up to a spot facing the lake, he was relieved to see that they were alone. He was glad because he and Jennifer needed to talk, really talk about some things. The setting was perfect with the full moon and all the stars reflected in the lake's waters. A breeze sprang up and added a shimmering effect to their glow. Trees stood like sentries around the lake, ready to protect anyone who stopped to admire the view.

He turned the radio on to a station that played soft music and then shifted to face Jennifer. She was sitting and watching him calmly with total trust in her eyes. At least he thought that was what he was reading in the look she was giving him.

He took one of her hands into his and began his speech. "Jennifer, I have something to tell you. We've been spending a lot of time together, and I think I'm falling in love with you. Do you think you could love me just a little?"

Jennifer took her time answering. He was beginning to get nervous. He hoped his palms wouldn't start sweating again. She looked him straight in the eye and replied, "Cody, I feel the same way. I didn't realize it until just now. I thought that we were just good friends, but you've been on my mind a lot lately." He had no idea of how much he had been in her thoughts, but that was her little secret, she reasoned.

He reached over and drew her closer for a kiss. She didn't resist, so that gave him hope. They kissed gently at first, and then their passion grew. He never wanted to let her go again.

She pulled back. "Cody, I can't breathe," she said breathlessly.

"I'm sorry. It's just that I didn't realize how much I cared for you until just now. Your kiss told me everything," he responded, his voice sounding a little husky.

"I think we need more time together," she said. "We don't get to talk much when we're out trapping cats. We have to be quiet."

"That doesn't stop me from looking at you," he said.

"I know. I've seen you stealing glances when you thought I wasn't looking. I was doing the same thing to you."

"So, what do you suggest?" he asked.

"Let's do something different. Spend some more time together away from other people."

"Okay, then, why don't you come to my apartment and I'll cook dinner for you?"

"I'd love that," she told him.

"So, how does a Saturday work for you?" he asked.

"Any Saturday would be just fine," she agreed.

It was then that he noticed he was still holding one of her hands. He brought it to his mouth and kissed it gently.

"It's a date. The first free Saturday we both have," he said. "Now I'd better get you home before those housemates of yours start calling your cell phone."

Jennifer laughed. "Yes, they are the nosy ones. I just hope they can find someone they're interested in when we have that fundraising party."

"I'll put the word out, and all the cops will show up," he promised.

They soon arrived at Jennifer's house, and Cody walked her to the door, as usual. This time, he didn't hesitate to kiss her again.

"I'll see you soon," he said.

Jennifer opened the door and walked into the house. Her housemates were watching TV, totally unaware of the scene they had just missed. It was better than a Hallmark movie. But she wasn't one to kiss and tell. She slipped up the stairs while they were still watching their show. She wasn't in the mood to talk to anybody else tonight.

Chapter 17

Sam and John had decided to take the morning off from tending yards and go fishing in the little creek that ran behind Miss Betty's house. They were on their spring break. They had promised to bring their Aunt Eliza some fish to cook for supper. Their luck had been good, and they had a string of fish to show for their efforts. They couldn't wait to get back to brag to Aunt Eliza and Uncle Jonas.

They rounded the corner of the trail that led to the creek and were about to pass by Miss Betty's house when they noticed a white van sitting in front of the driveway. They remembered the warnings from police bulletins to be on the lookout for suspicious vehicles.

"What do you suppose that van is doing in front of Miss Betty's house at this time of the morning?" John asked his brother.

"I don't know. We'd better be careful. Let's just stop and watch a while and see what happens," Sam told him.

They propped their fishing poles on the fence and hung the string of fish on a corner post of Miss Betty's yard and crouched behind the fence. Then they saw a man wearing a white uniform exit the van. He was carrying a toolbox. He walked up to the door and rang the doorbell. They saw Miss Betty open the door slightly and appear to be conversing with the man, who was waving his free hand excitedly as he spoke.

"What do you suppose he's saying?" John asked.

"I don't know, but it must be pretty important. He seems enthused about it," Sam responded. "Let's keep watching and see what happens next."

The man entered Miss Betty's house and was inside for a few minutes. Then he reappeared at the door and motioned for another man who had been sitting in the van to come to the house. The man got out and opened the back door of the van. They could see that it was filled with small animal cages.

"Oh, oh. That doesn't look good," said Sam. "Keep still and don't let them see you."

John backed further behind the fence, crawling backwards on his knees.

The men appeared at the door and looked around fervently before they exited the house, carrying the cages with them. It was obvious that the cages weren't empty.

"Oh, no. I think they got some of Miss Betty's cats! I hope Miss Betty's okay," Sam reported to John, who continued to crouch low to the ground.

It was about that time that one of the men looked their way as he scanned the neighborhood for anyone who might be watching them.

"Hey, Gus, I see a boy down there behind the fence," he shouted.

"Let's get him," Gus yelled back.

The boys began to run in the opposite direction, leaving all their fishing gear and their catch behind. They ran fast, but one of the men had turned the van around and was giving chase with it. As soon as it got even with them, a door opened, and the other man jumped out and grabbed John. Sam stopped because he couldn't leave his little brother behind.

He began yelling as loudly as he could. "Help, help! Somebody help us!"

By then the other man had jumped out and grabbed him. He stuffed a dirty rag in Sam's mouth. Sam almost gagged but stopped yelling.

Between them, the two men managed to wrestle the boys into the side door of the van. One of them grabbed two ropes and tied their hands and feet. The other one pulled out a half-clean handkerchief and tied it around John's mouth.

"Find me something to gag this other one with. He's gonna spit out the rag you stuffed in his mouth," said the one named Gus.

The other one pulled out a rag out of his back pocket and tied it around Sam's mouth.

"Let's hear you yell now," he said.

Both John and Sam quickly stopped struggling, realizing that they were in serious trouble.

"Just what we need. A couple of kids. What are we going to do with them now?" asked Gus.

"We've got no choice," replied the second man. "We've got to take them back with us. Otherwise, the whole operation is a bust."

Sam noticed that the name embroidered on his shirt said "Stan." Gus and Stan. He would definitely remember those two names if he and John ever got loose. He doubted if that was the guy's real name, though. Why would a criminal have his name embroidered on his shirt?

John was looking at his older brother with a completely terrified expression on his face. Sam shook his head slightly, indicating that John should be still and be quiet. Then he nodded toward the cages. They both could see Toby and some of Miss Betty's other cats in the cages. The rest of the cages held cats they didn't recognize. Now they were becoming part of the mystery, and they didn't like it. What was going to happen to them?

The van continued to travel at a rapid pace, leaving the neighborhood behind, but the boys had no idea of where they were headed, as it was a panel van with no rear windows. Now they knew why.

It was a bumpy ride, and they became more and more frightened wondering how they were going to get out of the mess they were in. Plus, what was going to become of the cats?

Chapter 18

Gloria arrived at her usual time to fix Miss Betty's lunch. She was surprised to find the door unlocked. She hurried inside and found Miss Betty tied up and lying on the floor with a rag fastened around her mouth. She had evidently passed out from the exhaustion of trying to free herself.

Gloria wasted no time in calling 9-1-1. She reported the incident as quickly as possible, requesting both a police car and an ambulance.

Several police cars arrived, lights flashing and sirens blaring. An ambulance was not far behind. People came out of their houses to view the scene. Miss Betty was a beloved member of their neighborhood, and they didn't want anything to happen to her. A crowd was starting to gather at the end of her sidewalk.

Two of the police officers who arrived were Cody and his partner, George. Cody knew he would have to let Jennifer know if anything had happened to Miss Betty because she and Miss Betty had become very close since Jennifer had started working with the TNR program.

"George, why don't you keep those people away from Miss Betty's house, and I'll go inside and see what I can find out?" Cody asked him.

"Sure thing, Cody. I hope Miss Betty's okay."

"Ditto for me, George."

Cody hurried up the walk after that remark as his partner headed towards the crowd. He had no doubt that George could disperse them in short order. He walked through the front door of the house and saw Miss Betty still lying on the floor. The EMT's had cut the ropes off her and removed the gag from around her mouth. Miss Betty was still unconscious and not looking good. One of them had placed an oxygen mask over her mouth and nose, while another one had hooked up an IV.

Gloria was standing close by and watching the whole process. She had started crying. Cody walked over to her while other police officers were searching the house and grounds.

"If only I had gotten here a little earlier," Gloria said between sobs. "I might have prevented the whole thing."

"Now, Gloria, don't go blaming yourself. We don't know exactly when it happened. It's probably a good thing you weren't here. You could have been injured, too. One thing's for sure. That cat nabbing ring is getting bolder, kidnapping cats in broad daylight. They must have heard about Miss Betty and all the cats she keeps in the house," Cody told her.

Just about that time, the EMT's were sliding Miss Betty onto a stretcher and preparing to take her outside to load her into the ambulance. Cody looked at Gloria to see how she was reacting. She seemed to be over her crying spell.

"Why don't you follow the ambulance to the hospital?" he asked. "That way, you won't be without a car like you would if you rode in the ambulance. I'm sure you can get an update on her condition, as she has no living kin, and you're her caretaker."

"Yes, she gave me power of attorney for her health care," Gloria told him. "She knew I would make the right decisions about her well-being."

"Great. I'm glad to know that. So, do you feel up to driving yourself to the hospital now?"

"Yes, I'll make it. I feel a lot calmer now that she's off that floor. I just hope she didn't fall and hit her head or break something."

"From the looks of things, I'd say the intruders tied her up and left her sitting on the floor. I think she fell over when she tried to get untied," Cody decided as he looked over the scene.

Gloria headed out to her car, while Cody joined the rest of the police officers who had been surveying the inside of the house for clues. They had taken fingerprints, but none turned up except for those obviously belonging to Miss Betty and her usual visitors, leading them to conclude that the perps must have been wearing gloves.

Several of the officers had checked the garden, and one went to look around the outside of Miss Betty's fence. He noticed the two fishing poles leaning against the fence and the string of fish hooked to the corner post.

"Hey, guys, over here," he yelled. "I think I've found something."

The other officers hurried to the spot where the officer was standing. He pointed to the fishing poles and string of fish.

"What do you make of this?" he asked.

"Looks like someone's fishing trip got interrupted," another one said.

"I wonder who it was," a third officer mused.

Cody took in the scene and an idea came to him. "You know, I believe that those poles just might belong to Jonas Green's great-nephews," he told them. "I know that they've been helping Jonas with his gardening chores for Miss Betty's yard. They knew the creek ran behind her house, and they just might have decided to have themselves an early morning fishing trip."

"Looks like they had pretty good luck with that," the first officer observed.

"Yes, but maybe not such good luck with the cat nabbers, if that's who tied up Miss Betty," said Cody.

"Look here in the dirt. Looks like one of them was kneeling and trying to hide," said one of the officers.

"Yes, I see that," Cody observed as he looked more closely. "I'm guessing it was the younger one, John. His big brother, Sam, would have tried to protect him."

Sergeant Phillips joined the men who had congregated at the fence line. "What's going on here?" he asked.

"We think that some kids have been kidnapped, along with the cats," Cody told him.

Sergeant Phillips' face began to turn red, a sure sign that his temper was about to flare. All of the men took a step back, each hoping they wouldn't be the target of his wrath. He began to speak.

"That does it! I've had it with these cat nabbers and now kidnappers. Get out there and talk to everyone in every house on this street and find out if anybody saw or heard anything. I'm going to track those suckers down if it's the last thing I do, and it just might be if I don't find my wife's cat."

The men scattered, thankful that none of them had been directly addressed by Sergeant Phillips.

Chapter 19

The police officers wasted no time in following Sergeant Phillips' orders. They divided into pairs and went up and down the street, questioning anyone who might be at home. They were able to glean a little information from a couple of the neighbors. One of them had seen a white van parked in front of Miss Betty's house, and another peeked out her window and had seen two men carrying something from Miss Betty's house and putting it in the van. The second witness couldn't be sure, but she thought it looked like cages with animals inside. She said she didn't call the police because she wasn't sure of what she had seen.

Cody was almost beside himself with anxiety when he heard that information. His instincts had been right! The white van was the key to whatever had been happening around town with all the animal disappearances. The question was, how had the vehicle managed to disappear so conveniently every time he had spotted it? There had to be a headquarters hidden somewhere in the community. Plus, if the

Greens' boys had been taken, why had that happened? The mystery was deepening.

He knew he had to let Jennifer know about Miss Betty being attacked and now being taken to the hospital in an ambulance. He pulled his cell phone out of his pocket to make the call.

Jennifer picked up on the first ring as soon as she saw Cody's name and number come up. She was on duty at the firehouse, but nothing was happening at the moment.

"Hello, Cody," she answered. "What's up?"

"I'm afraid I have some bad news for you," he told her. "We found Miss Betty collapsed and tied up on the floor of her house. She was unconscious, so an ambulance is taking her to the hospital. They're probably already there."

"Oh, no! Not Miss Betty, my sweet Miss Betty. Why in the world would anybody want to hurt Miss Betty?" Cody detected a trace of tears in her voice as she spoke.

"There's more to the story. All of her cats are missing. Some of the neighbors think they saw them being carried out of the house in cages."

"All of them? Even Toby?" Jennifer inquired anxiously.

"Yes, I'm sorry to say that Toby is among the missing cats," he replied.

"What can I do to help?" she asked.

"The police are handling the case. Gloria went to the hospital to be with Miss Betty. If there's any way you can get away from work, I think it would be a good idea for you to go and be with Gloria. She's pretty upset because she was the one who found Miss Betty on the floor."

"I'll try to get away," Jennifer promised. "I have some leave time coming. Since this is an emergency, I'll ask the chief to let me go and be with both of them."

"Thanks. I feel a lot better about it. The case is more complicated than I can talk about right now. I'll fill you in on the details after the police department releases the information."

"Okay, I'll be waiting to hear from you," Jennifer said as she touched her phone to end the call.

She immediately headed to the chief's office to plead her case. The chief was very understanding and immediately agreed that Jennifer going to be with Gloria and Miss Betty at the hospital was the right thing to do. She headed to the locker room and changed from her firefighter's pants and tee-shirt to her casual clothes.

Her change in appearance was not unnoticed by her fellow firefighters as she walked back through the lounge, heading outside to her car.

"Hey, Jennifer, what's going on?" Freddy asked as soon as she entered the room.

"Yeah, it's your turn to cook," Don reminded her.

"I'm sorry, guys, but something very important has come up. I can't talk about it now, but I'll fill you in on it later," she told them as she headed out the door.

The guys looked at each other, totally puzzled.

"That was strange," said Calvin.

"Sure was," Freddy agreed.

"I'm getting hungry already. So which one of you guys is going to fill in as the cook for the day?" Calvin asked.

"I think we should be more worried about what's going on with Jennifer. She didn't even give us a hint of where she's going or why she's leaving. It must be something serious," Don told them.

"You're right. I need to think about something other than my stomach," Calvin admitted. "I guess I'll fill in and do the cooking. It's the least I can do, especially since I'm always the one who's the hungriest."

Everyone had to laugh at that remark, although they were a little concerned, as Calvin was not known for his cooking skills.

All thoughts of food were banished as the fire alarm went off, and they went into their firefighters' mode, slipping into their gear and hopping into the trucks to answer the call.

Chapter 20

Jennifer drove as fast as she dared to get to the hospital. She walked up to the reception desk and inquired about Miss Betty and Gloria. The receptionist informed her that Gloria was sitting in the ICU waiting room. Jennifer hurried into the elevator and hit the button to the third floor, where the ICU was located.

She walked into the waiting room and spotted Gloria immediately. Gloria's face had been streaked with tears, as was evident by her ruined mascara. Jennifer felt sorry for her because she knew that Gloria regarded Miss Betty as somewhat of a mother figure, having no family of her own.

Gloria looked up as Jennifer entered the room and motioned for Jennifer to come over and join her on the couch where she was sitting.

"Jennifer, I'm so glad you came," Gloria told her. "I'm so worried about Miss Betty. She still hasn't regained consciousness."

"Oh, no. That's not good for a woman her age," Jennifer commented.

"No, it's not. The doctors say if she doesn't regain consciousness soon, she might not ever wake up." Gloria choked up as she spoke.

Jennifer's eyes filled with tears as she heard the news. She couldn't believe that something like this was happening in Summerfield, especially to someone as good and kind as Miss Betty.

"We have to get her back," Jennifer told Gloria. "Who else is going to be our unofficial matchmaker for all the young people?"

Gloria smiled sadly. "You're right. Miss Betty certainly knows how to get couples together. If I'm not mistaken, you and Cody are one of her latest projects." She wiped her eyes as she spoke.

"I kind of suspected that," Jennifer admitted. "But you know what? I didn't mind at all. Cody is such a nice guy. He's been a lot of help to me in trapping those feral cats. I couldn't have done it by myself. I think he has more patience than I do."

"That probably comes from his being a police officer. They have to be very patient with people sometimes and also do a lot of waiting if they're on a stakeout."

"Yes, they do. I hadn't really thought much about it. Cody doesn't talk about his work a lot. I guess he has to keep a lot of the information confidential," Jennifer said.

"Miss Betty told me that she had high hopes for you and Cody becoming a real couple," Gloria informed her. "She's not wrong very often."

"I think her plan just might be working," Jennifer confided.

"I'm glad," Gloria said. "It's just too bad she never found anybody for me."

"Well, you never know. There might be somebody out there. New people are always coming to Summerfield," Jennifer noted.

"You're right, but it's not the end of the world if I stay single. What I'm most worried about now is Miss Betty and her cats."

"Oh, yes, the cats. Cody told me that they had all been taken. Poor

Toby. He'll be so lost without Miss Betty. I hope they can find all of them unharmed.

"So do I, and I just hope they can solve the mystery of why all of the cats have been disappearing," said Gloria.

"Summerfield has a great police department, even if it is a small town. I'm sure Cody's dad will make sure they do everything they can to get the cats home again," Jennifer assured her.

A nurse appeared in the doorway of the waiting room and asked Gloria to follow her for a conference with the doctor.

"I'd like Jennifer to come with me," Gloria told her.

"No problem," the nurse replied. "You have the power of attorney, so if you want Jennifer with you, it's fine."

They followed the nurse back to a conference room where she asked them to be seated to wait for the doctor. He entered the room several minutes later, a somber look on his face.

"Doctor, what can you tell us about Miss Betty's condition now?" Gloria asked.

"I'm sorry to say that there's been no change. She's still unconscious. We're keeping her hydrated and also sedated so that her body can mend. It appears that she hit her head when she fell over on the floor. We've done a CT scan, and we don't see any serious damage. Fortunately, she didn't fall very far, from what I've been told, as she was already sitting on the floor. Still, at her age, no hit on the head is good. She's breathing on her own. That's a good sign. We're still waiting to see if she wakes up."

"We'll pray for her," Jennifer interjected.

"Could we see her now?" Gloria asked.

"Yes, you may go in for a couple of minutes, but that's all," the doctor said.

"We'll do that, and then we'll go to the chapel to pray," Gloria decided.

"Yes, that's a splendid idea," Jennifer agreed.

"Good," the doctor said. "I'll let you know if her condition changes."

He held the door open for them to exit. They headed to Miss Betty's room, while he continued on his rounds.

Chapter 21

Cody had been busy after the police wrapped up their investigation at the crime scene. Sergeant Phillips had given him and George the assignment of reporting the kidnapping of John and Sam to their family. They were on their way to the Greens' house with Cody wondering just how he was going to break the news to Jonas, Eliza, Adolphus, and his wife, Emma.

"George, this isn't going to be easy," Cody commented as they neared the houses, which were located beside each other. "I just hope somebody is home to receive the news."

"Yes, the men are always busy with their gardening chores," George said. "I've even had them do my yard a few times when I was too busy to do it myself. They're excellent workers."

"I see Jonas's truck in his driveway," Cody observed as they pulled up beside the curb.

"I hope seeing a police car doesn't scare them too much," George added as they exited the car.

They walked up Jonas's sidewalk and knocked on the door. They could hear a TV droning in the background.

Cody rang the doorbell, and Jonas opened the door, a look of surprise on his face.

"What you two guys doin' here?" he asked. "Is somethin' wrong?"

"Hello, Jonas. May we come in?" Cody asked.

"Why, sure, Cody, come on in. Eliza is just makin' some lunch for me. It's my day off," Jonas told him.

"This is my partner, George," Cody told him as they walked into the living room.

"Good to meet you, George. I think I've seen you at church," Jonas said.

"Yes, we do attend the same church. I'm not there a lot because of my police duties," George explained.

"Have a seat. Can I get you two guys a glass of sweet tea? Eliza makes some mighty good tea," Jonas offered.

"Thanks, Jonas, that sounds delicious," Cody told him.

"Liza, we got company. Can you bring two glasses of your sweet tea out here?" Jonas yelled towards the kitchen.

Eliza poked her head around the corner of the door and looked slightly shocked to see two police officers sitting in her living room. She hurriedly fetched two glasses from the cabinet, filled them with ice, and poured the tea for the visitors.

"Here you go," she said, as she brought the tea into the living room.

"So, why are you here?" Jonas asked. "Did somethin' happen to Miss Betty?" He sounded a little anxious. Eliza didn't look much better. She knew that having two police officers come to their house couldn't be a good thing.

George started the explanation. "I'm afraid we have some bad news for you and also for Adolphus and Emma."

"Bad news? Whatcha mean?" Jonas exclaimed.

"We believe that John and Sam have been kidnapped," Cody told them.

Eliza burst into tears. "Oh, no. My sweet boys. Who would want to do that?" She continued to sob as Jonas rose and put his arm around her shoulders.

"Now, Liza, let the men talk. Tell us what happened," he said.

"Something has happened to Miss Betty and her cats. Gloria found Miss Betty tied up and collapsed on the floor, and all the cats are gone," Cody explained gently.

"Miss Betty tied up. Is she okay? What does that have to do with our boys?" Jonas asked."

"Miss Betty was carried to the hospital by ambulance," Cody told him.

George gave further information. "We found some fishing poles and a line of fish tied to Miss Betty's fence post. We think they belonged to the boys."

"Yes, they did say that they were goin' fishin' this morning. We were supposed to have a fish supper. It was goin' to be a surprise for Adolphus and Emma," Jonas told them.

"I knew something would happen. I wish you had gone with them now," Eliza said, still sobbing as she spoke.

"Now, Liza. Those boys have been fishin' plenty of times. Nothin' ever happened to them before. Summerfield has always been a safe place to live," Jonas said.

"Well, it's not so safe now!" she exclaimed. "How do we get our boys back?"

"We're working on it," Cody explained. "We've canvassed the neighborhood and gathered some clues. We just have more investigation to do. I want you two to stay calm and stay at home. Is Adolphus at home now?"

"No, he's working," Eliza said.

"Well, if you can call him on his cell phone, I would suggest that you call him and let him know right away. What about Emma?" Cody asked.

"She's working at a beauty shop. She does the braids for the lady who owns the shop," Eliza explained.

"You should call her, too," George said. "Both parents need to come home and wait until we have an update on the situation."

"I'll call them both," Jonas decided. "Liza is too upset to do it."

"Okay, I'm counting on you, then," Cody told him. He turned to Eliza. "Thank you so much for the tea, Eliza. Jonas was right. You do make delicious sweet tea."

Eliza smiled a little and dabbed at her eyes with her apron. "I think that's one reason Jonas married me. I'm a good cook, and I make great tea."

"Oh, Liza, you know it was more than that," Jonas countered. "Now don't you guys worry. I'll make the phone calls, and I know Adolphus and Emma will come right home."

"Good. Stay near the phone. I promise to let you know the minute I learn something," Cody promised. "George, I guess we'd better get back on duty before Sergeant Phillips starts summoning us to another crime scene."

"Yes, you're right. It was good meeting both of you, although it wasn't under the happiest of circumstances. Just put your trust in God and pray about it. Remember all of those sermons Pastor Sices has been preaching. Why don't you call him and start a prayer chain?" George asked.

"That's a good idea. I'll do that, too," Jonas said. "Yes, sir. Prayer can't hurt a thing. We'll put our trust in God and have a prayer as soon as you leave."

"Don't forget about the calls," Cody reminded him as he and George exited the door.

"Oh, yes. I'll do that right away. When Adolphus and Emma arrive, we'll all pray together."

Cody and George walked back to their police cruiser and climbed inside. The radio was crackling.

"Oh, brother, I hope that's not Sergeant Phillips looking for us," Cody said.

"At least we can give him a report of what we learned about the boys," George noted.

"Yes, you're right. I just hope we can get them back safely. Somehow and someway, we've got to locate those cat nabbers. That's where the boys will be," Cody mused as he started the car and put it into gear. He pulled back onto the street slowly, his mind filled with thoughts of the cat nabbers, the kidnapped boys, Miss Betty lying in a hospital bed, and Jennifer and Gloria by her side. There would be no rest for anybody until those boys were found and the cat nabbers were brought to justice.

Chapter 22

Sam and John had no idea of how long they had been riding in the van. They had felt themselves going around a lot of curves and over a lot of bumps. The road seemed to be getting bumpier by the minute. It was obvious that they had left a paved road and were now on some kind of gravel or dirt road. The driver had slowed down considerably.

There was very little conversation between their captors, leading Sam to believe that he and John were to be kept from learning too much information. He just hoped it wouldn't turn out badly in the end for both them and the cats in the van.

They felt the van stop briefly and heard the sound of an automatic garage door going up, and then they felt van a dip as they went down a steep incline. The vehicle came to a halt, and the captors climbed out, leaving Sam, John, and the captured cats inside it. Without warning, the overhead lights in the room came on, indicating that one of the two men had flipped a light switch. Sam nodded to John as a signal that they should try to get free from the ropes that were binding them.

They scooted close together, with little room left to maneuver among the cages of cats, some of whom were meowing loudly.

Sam began trying to loosen John's rope that was tying his hands behind his back, but with little success. The knots were tight, and the rope was stiff. John shook his head as an indication that Sam pulling on the rope was hurting his wrists, so Sam decided it was best to give up that task for the time being.

Suddenly, the van doors opened, and the two men reappeared. They began removing the cages of cats and carrying them to one side of what appeared to be an underground storage facility. The boys could see that other cats were already there, stacked in cages. Some were sleeping, while others huddled in fear in the back of their cages. Sam felt sorry for them, but not as sorry as he felt for himself and his brother. He knew he had to do everything in his power to protect his younger brother.

After the cats had been unloaded, the men reappeared and looked at the boys. The gleam in their eyes was not a pleasant one, by any means. It was obvious that they were unhappy to have the boys as company on their mission, whatever it might be.

The one named Gus began to talk. "Let's get these kids out of the van. We'll put them over in that far corner on the floor. They should be okay for a while."

"But what are we going to do with them?" asked the one with "Stan" embroidered on his shirt.

"I'll figure that out later. I need to call the boss first," Gus told him.

They each grabbed hold of one of the boys and half-lifted and half-dragged them out of the van roughly. They then placed them on the floor in the corner Gus had indicated, dropping them as they let go of their hold on them.

John moaned as he hit the floor, but Sam managed to remain quiet, determined to set an example of courage for his younger brother. They both squirmed enough to get themselves in an upright sitting position with their backs against the cold wall.

Sam managed to catch his brother's attention as John stared at him through frightened eyes. Sam raised his chin and rolled his eyes towards the ceiling as a sign that they should begin to pray. John understood after Sam repeated the motion several times.

Both boys bowed their heads and closed their eyes and began to pray silently. The gags were still over their mouths, so they couldn't speak to communicate.

After a time, Sam nudged John as a sign that they should stop praying and look around their surroundings. Gus was on his cell phone, talking in low tones. Stan was pacing the floor and smoking a cigarette. A trail of cigarette butts lined the floor, showing where he had walked.

"Hurry up, can't you?" Stan asked Gus, who waved him off as he continued to talk on the cell phone. Finally, he ended the call.

So, what's the plan?" Stan asked. "When can we get these cats off our hands? I'm ready to blow this town. I didn't like those cops who stopped us the other day. They were way too curious."

"You're right, but now that we left an old lady tied up in her house, all the cops are going to be looking for us. We've got to start moving these cats out of here now," Gus told him.

"What about the kids?" Stan asked.

"I think we'll just leave them here. They can't get away, so they can't do much about their situation. It'll be a long time before anybody finds them," Gus said.

Sam and John overheard that part of the conversation. Sam knew they were in real trouble. He just hoped that the men would leave them alive and that somehow they would be able to get free afterwards. He shook his head at John to be quiet and still.

The men began to load the cages into the van. It was a tight fit, but they got every last cage in. The cats were not happy about being jostled around, and some of them were yowling.

"Dang those cats! I wish they would shut up!" Stan complained.

"They'll be quiet enough as soon as the van starts moving. It seems to soothe them," Gus told him.

"Well, let's get on the road. We have to take the backroads because the cops probably have all the main highways blocked," Gus said. He seemed to be the brains of the two, Sam decided, as he listened to the conversation.

Gus got into the van and started it, and Stan turned out the overhead lights, using a flashlight to make his way to the van. One of them hit the remote-controlled door opener, and the vehicle headed up the sharp incline. As soon as it reached the top, the door closed, and Sam and John were alone in the dark.

Their eyes slowly adjusted to the darkness, and Sam heard a small mini-refrigerator running on the other side of the large room. He started working his way across the room until he reached it. He managed to pull the door open, and light poured forth from the small bulb inside it.

Sam looked around for something to cut the ropes with. The men hadn't left much behind. There were a couple of soft drinks inside the refrigerator, but there was no food. He realized that the soft drinks could come in handy to keep them hydrated.

John was still sitting by the other wall watching all his brother's actions. He looked a little happier when he spotted the soft drinks. Sam realized that John didn't know they would have to ration the liquid if they wanted to survive.

Sam worked his way back over to John and managed to get himself positioned face-to-face with his brother. He indicated that his brother should hold still while he tried to remove the gag from his mouth using his teeth. It took several tries, but he was finally successful.

John drew a long, deep breath before he spoke. "Thanks, Sam. I could hardly breathe. Let me get yours off."

He proceeded to remove his brother's gag the same way, and Sam spat out the offending dirty rag that had been crammed into his mouth. He, too, took a deep breath, relishing the first fresh air he had taken in since the gag had been tied on him.

"Now we can talk," he told John. "We have to get these ropes loose. I don't think those men are coming back because they took all the cats with them."

"I don't think so either," said John. "I wish they hadn't taken Miss Betty's cats."

"Me, too, but there's nothing we can do about that now. I hope they didn't hurt Miss Betty. Let's look around and see if we can find anything to pry these knots loose."

They both looked around as best they could in the dim light provided by the refrigerator. It was then that Sam spotted it—a small knife that had been overlooked by the two kidnappers. It was lying beside some dried-up apple peelings on the floor. That proved they weren't very smart, he thought.

"Look, do you see that little knife under the table? Maybe we can use it to cut the ropes loose," he told John.

"I hope so. They're making my wrists and ankles hurt," John complained.

"Let's work our way over to where the knife is, and then we'll figure out what to do," said Sam.

The boys began squirming across the floor, intent on reaching the knife and hoping that they had seen the last of Gus and Stan. They managed to reach the knife but had trouble figuring out how to hold it with their hands tied behind their backs.

"I've got an idea," said Sam. "It's a little dangerous, though. I'll do the hard part, but you have to stay perfectly still. Do you trust me?"

"I always trust you, Sam, even though you do play tricks on me sometimes."

"Well, this is no trick. It's for real. If you move, one of us could get hurt. I'm going to try to cut your rope loose holding the handle of the knife in my mouth. Do you think you can be still?"

"Sure, I can be still if I have to," John replied.

Sam lay down in the floor and carefully began to maneuver in the right direction to situate himself to put the knife handle across his mouth. It took several tries, but he finally managed to grasp it using his teeth. He wriggled over behind John and raised his head slightly to get the knife in the right position. He very slowly lowered it until it touched the rope. He hoped John wouldn't move. He began using a sawing motion and could see that a few strands of the rope loosened. It wasn't easy because the movements were beginning to blister the sides of his mouth.

"Is it working?" John asked.

"Uh-huh," Sam managed to mumble. He went back to sawing on the rope. He wished he knew what time it was because it seemed like he had been trying to cut the rope for an hour. He knew it couldn't have been that long. He stopped to rest and catch his breath.

"Why did you stop?" John asked.

"Tired," he managed to mumble again. By then the sides of his mouth were bleeding, but he knew he couldn't stop, and he couldn't ask his little brother to undertake such a task. He had to be the big brother now. It was all up to him.

Finally, he had gotten about three-fourths of the way through one strand of the rope. His neck hurt, and his mouth was still bleeding. He had to go on. He rested for a while again, and then he resumed his task. At last, he hit the final strand, and the rope broke loose.

He spit out the knife. "Try now," he told John, who immediately began to wave his hands in the air.

"Oh, boy, you did it, Sam! You really did it!"

John turned around to look at his big brother with all the blood coming from the sides of his mouth. His eyes grew wider as he took in the scene and realized just how much of a sacrifice Sam had made to free him.

"Oh, no. You're hurt!" he exclaimed.

"Never mind that. Get the rest of the rope off yourself and then untie me or cut the rope off me, whichever works best for you," Sam told him.

John made short work of removing both ropes. Then he looked longingly at the two soft drinks in the refrigerator.

"Do you suppose we could have those drinks now?" he asked hopefully.

"We can open one of them and each drink a swallow. We have to ration them because we don't know how long we'll be stuck here," Sam explained. "Do you see anything I could use to wipe this blood off my face first?"

John looked around the dimly lit room. Then he looked back at Sam.

"I don't see anything," he said.

"Well, help me tear off a piece of my shirt, and I'll use that," Sam decided. "It's probably cleaner than anything in here anyhow."

After Sam's wounds had been blotted clean, he stood up and walked to the minifridge. He took out one of the soft drinks and opened it slowly. He handed it to John. "Remember, just one swallow," he reminded John.

John followed his orders and handed the drink back to him. "It's your turn now," he said.

Sam took one swallow of the soda and placed it back in the mini-fridge. "It's not going to stay cold with that door open, but it's the only light we have. I might be able to find the light switch, but what if the guys come back? We'd better just stick with what we have. If you aren't scared of the dark, we can sit close to the refrigerator and close it for a little while."

"Let's do that," John agreed. "I'm not scared of the dark. Remember when we used to chase all of those fireflies?"

"Yes, those were the good old days," Sam said, feeling a little older now.

"I'm so tired, Sam. Do you think it would be all right if I took a little nap?" John asked.

"Sure, little brother. You go ahead and sleep. I'll keep watch in case those bad men come back," Sam told him. He was feeling a little sleepy himself. After all, they had gotten up early to go fishing. He really wished he was eating some of that fish now with his family around him.

John dozed off, and Sam smiled. He was feeling very much like a big brother again. His eyelids began to droop, and soon he, too, was fast asleep.

Chapter 23

The whole town of Summerfield was abuzz with the news of cats disappearing, Miss Betty being tied up and found unconscious, and the Greens' boys missing. The phones in the police stations were ringing constantly with people who thought they had spotted a white van, more cats reported missing, and some calls that led nowhere.

Jake Hawthorne, the police chief, was overseeing the entire operation non-stop. Both Cody and Jake's wife, Jillian, were worried about him putting in so many hours without a break. However, he was determined to solve the case and get the cats back to their rightful owners. He was especially concerned about Miss Betty's cats and hoped that they would be found soon.

Jake had directed Sergeant Phillips to have roadblocks set up on all the roads leading out of town. They also had officers on guard at the bus station and also at the airport in Brooksville, their sister city across the river, just in case the crooks decided to abandon the cats and make a run for it. So far, nothing had turned up, and there had been no further signs of the mysterious white van.

Gloria and Jennifer had been keeping watch over Miss Betty, going into the ICU every time visitors were allowed. There was no change in her condition. No one else was allowed to see her, but many of her friends came to the ICU waiting room to talk to Gloria and Jennifer. Several of Miss Betty's best friends convinced them to go home for a shower and change of clothes. They left reluctantly but realizing that the advice was good and well-intentioned.

Gloria and Jennifer chatted as they walked towards the entrance of the hospital.

"If I ever get my hands on whoever did this to Miss Betty, they will be very sorry," Gloria said.

"I don't think you'll get a chance for that because by the time Sergeant Phillips gets through with them, there won't be much for anybody else to work over," Jennifer told her.

"Oh, I know he'd love to do that, but he'll operate within the law. He's been a police officer for too long. I'm sure Chief Hawthorne will make sure that they'll be behind bars for a long time," Gloria replied.

"No doubt about it. Kidnapping is a serious felony. Taking the cats was bad enough, but the kidnappers also took two kids. I just hope the boys will be unharmed and will be located soon."

"Yes, I heard that Jonas' church organized a prayer chain. Maybe we should do something like that at our church."

"I'll call the pastor and see if we can have a prayer session or something," Jennifer said.

They reached their cars and both headed home for the shower and change of clothes. Jennifer reached her house to find her two housemates there with a meal prepared for her.

"How did you know to cook for me?" she asked.

"One of the ladies phoned us from the ICU waiting room and suggested it, so we hopped right on it," Laura told her.

"Why don't you take a shower and change clothes, and we'll get the food on the table?" Donna suggested.

"Good idea. I can't wait to feel that warm water running over me," said Jennifer as she climbed the stairs.

"I guess she has something to think about besides Cody," Laura observed as they watched her heading for her room.

"Not for too long," Donna said. "I know that girl and how she thinks, and she thinks about Cody a lot now."

"Yes, they really are a couple, and you and I are still both single and looking," said Laura as she let out a sigh.

"Well, don't forget. It's almost time for the fundraising party. I think we need to start the ads on the radio and Facebook and start gathering our supplies. After all, if we want to have a Maypole, it should be on May Day," Donna reminded her.

"Yes, maybe if we talk to Jennifer about that, it will help keep her mind off Miss Betty," Laura noted.

They hurried to set the table and began to bring the food in. They had just set the glasses of iced tea into place when Jennifer reappeared, looking a little fresher and wearing different clothes.

"Oh, gosh! I never realized a shower could feel so good!" Jennifer exclaimed as she took her seat at the table.

Donna evaluated her looks and gave a report of what she saw. "You have circles under your eyes. You and Gloria need to take turns staying at the hospital at nights so you can get some sleep."

"That's a good idea. I'll talk to Gloria about it when we both get back to the hospital. It'll be hard to get Gloria to leave for very long, though," Jennifer told them.

They dug into the food after saying a blessing. "I'm so glad I picked housemates who can both cook," Jennifer commented. "It's good to have some homemade food again after surviving that cafeteria food."

Donna and Laura both shook their heads and gave disgusted looks at the mention of cafeteria food.

"And those firefighters should be glad you can cook," Laura reminded Jennifer.

"Oh, they are. Somehow, it seems to be my turn to cook more often than their turns. We try to skip Calvin when we can, as his cooking skills aren't the best," Jennifer commented.

"Can't he cook anything? I thought firefighters were supposed to be good cooks. After all, there are quite a few firefighters' cookbooks out there. I've read a few of them, and the recipes sound pretty good," Donna said.

"Well, he's pretty good with peanut-butter-and-jelly sandwiches," Jennifer said, chuckling as she spoke. "Sometimes he even toasts the bread."

"He really goes all out, then," Laura said. "What he needs is a woman who can cook."

"He *is* single," Jennifer told her.

"Hmm…guess I'll check him out at the May Day fundraising," Laura mused.

"Say, what are you trying to do—replace Miss Betty as the town's matchmaker?" Donna asked.

"Well, you girls have been complaining about being dateless. No time like the present to start looking," Jennifer noted.

"You just be sure some of those firefighters and police officers show up!" Donna exclaimed.

"Don't worry. Cody has assured me that he will have all the eligible policemen there," Jennifer told them. "However, don't forget that the main reason for the event is to raise money for the TNR program, not to find potential husbands."

"You're right," Donna admitted. "But it can't hurt to kill two birds with one stone, as the old saying goes."

"Yes, we can do some 'window shopping' while we're raising money," Laura agreed.

"I just hope it's a success both with raising money and everyone having a good time. I think everybody will be in the mood for a celebration after this cat nabbing mystery is solved and the boys are found and brought home. I just hope that God will keep all of them safe until then," said Jennifer as she finished off the last bite of her meal.

Chapter 24

Both Chief Hawthorne and Sergeant Phillips were beginning to grow frustrated because the roadblocks had not turned up any trace of the cat nabbers or the kidnapped boys. An APB had been issued on the van for the surrounding counties, and all police departments were on the lookout for it. So far, nobody had seen it again.

"That van has to be somewhere in this area," Sergeant Phillips told his chief. "They haven't had time to get far."

"Perhaps they holed up somewhere," Chief Hawthorne mused. "I wonder where a good hiding place would be."

"We've already searched all the warehouses and deserted houses in the area," Sergeant Phillips informed him. "We came up with nothing."

"Well, think. Is there any place you could have missed? Any place at all? What about somewhere farther out of town?" the chief asked.

"We'll broaden the search area," Sergeant Phillips said. "I'll get right on it."

He immediately called a meeting of the detective squad and police officers on duty and informed them of the plan. No house was to be left unsearched, no matter how bad its condition. He emphasized that time was of the essence because of the safety of the boys and the health of the cats. Everyone present agreed with him and left immediately to begin searching more deserted houses, even those that were located out of town.

They had just about exhausted the search when one of the detectives remembered a house that had been deserted for a long time. A couple with the last name of Harris, who had owned it, were practically hermits and lived far off the road with just a small gravel trail leading through the woods to the house. They had no children and had long since passed away, so there was nobody to inherit the property. Rumor was that they had left its profits to charity. It had been up for sale several times with no takers.

The detective and his partner followed the trail, which grew smaller as they entered the woods, and one of them noticed some fresh tire tracks in the spots where the gravel had disappeared.

"Looks like somebody has been here recently," he commented to his partner. "Let's call for backup."

"Good idea," the other one agreed. He put out the call on the police radio, and Cody responded that he was close by and would be there right away. Several other cars followed suit, and soon a line of police cars with flashing lights was headed towards the deserted and dilapidated house. They didn't turn on their sirens just in case the kidnappers were still in the house.

The first car pulled into what used to be the yard but was now overgrown with weeds and some small trees. The two detectives waited for the rest of the group to arrive. It didn't take long. Soon, the entire space was filled with police cars.

Everyone exited the cars and grouped behind the lead car. They couldn't see any light coming from the house. It appeared that nobody was there. Everything was quiet except for an unexplained humming sound that was coming from the back side of the house.

"Let's split up and search around the house," Cody suggested. He and George paired off, as did the rest of the group. Cody ran his light over the outside of the house as he and George carefully made their way towards what appeared to be an old driveway.

"Do you see that?" he asked George, as he shined the light on a newly installed garage door.

"Yes, it looks like somebody was here and put in a new garage door," George responded.

By then, the other cops and detectives had made their way around the house and were approaching the driveway. Cody motioned to them to be quiet as they crept up towards the door. Everything was still totally dark inside.

"We have something to report," one of the policemen told Cody. "We found a portable generator running in the back. If nobody's in the house, I guess somebody forgot to turn it off unless they plan on coming back."

"Yes, nobody has lived here for years. It had to be somebody who was camped out here," Cody said. "It was probably those cat nabbers. They must have scouted the area and found this house to use as their headquarters. There was little chance of them being seen here, as nobody comes this way anymore."

"I wonder if there's any way we can get this door open," said George.

"It looks pretty tightly sealed to me, and I don't see any windows at this part of the house, either," Cody commented.

"It appears to be an underground garage. I guess the owners didn't trust leaving their vehicles at ground level," one of the cops noted.

"The couple who owned it were known for being a little strange.

My dad wouldn't let me come trick-or-treating here when I was a kid," Cody told them.

"I wonder if anybody's in there," said another cop.

"We have to figure out a way to get in," Cody mused. "I don't think the kidnappers are here because we haven't seen a single sign of light anywhere. I know they wouldn't be sitting in the dark."

"There might not even be anybody inside," George observed. "If they were there, they're probably gone now."

"Only one way to find out," Cody decided. "We have to get that door open. Some of you guys get a pry bar or something to open it with."

A couple of the detectives went to fetch their pry bars and returned shortly with them in hand.

"Who's brave enough to start prying on this door?" Cody asked.

"I'll do it," said George.

"I'll help," added one of the cops.

They began slowly working around the edges of the door, trying to loosen it. Suddenly, they saw a glimmer of light coming from underneath the door.

"Hold it!" Cody ordered. "Somebody just turned a light on. There's somebody in there."

That's when they heard the cries for help. They weren't very loud, but someone was definitely calling for help.

"It sounds like the missing boys," said Cody. "Forget prying the door open. Let's just smash it open with one of the police cars."

"Okay, who wants to be the victim of Sergeant Phillips' wrath when their cruiser needs repair?" one of them joked.

"I'll do it," George volunteered again. He headed back to the cruiser he and Cody had been using, started it, and the headlights came on. He slowly lined up the car with the door and paused.

"Be careful. That garage is underground. It has to be a steep incline.

You don't want to go down into the garage. Don't give it too much gas," Cody cautioned.

George slowly accelerated the vehicle until it hit the garage door, which collapsed under the impact of the hit. He quickly pushed on the brakes and barely kept the car from going into the garage. The dim light showed two figures lined up beside one of the walls. One was a head taller than the other one.

Cody and the others approached slowly, guns in hand, scouring the area with their flashlights.

"Sam, John, is that you?" he called out.

"Yes, it's us. Mr. Cody, is that you? We've been waiting for somebody to find us. We couldn't get out by ourselves," Sam told him.

By then, one of the cops had located the main light switch and flipped it on. They all took in the scene that showed a hurried departure.

"So, what happened?" Cody asked them. "Are you two all right?"

"Yes, we're a little cold and thirsty. However, we're okay," said Sam.

"Sam found the refrigerator and some sodas for us, but he wouldn't let me drink much at a time," John explained.

"That was smart of him," Cody noted.

"We sure are hungry," Sam said. "We were planning on having a fish dinner. We ended up being kidnapped instead."

"So, can you describe the people who did it?" asked one of the detectives, who had taken out his notebook.

"It was two men. They had a lot of cats. We saw them at Miss Betty's house, and then they chased us down the street," Sam told him.

"Yeah, and they caught us and tied us up," John added.

"We were pretty scared, but they decided to leave us. They loaded up all the cats in their van, and then they left us in the dark, still tied up. I think their names were Gus and Stan," said Sam.

"Gus and Stan…that's a start, anyhow," the detective told them.

"Those are the names on the I.D.'s of two guys Cody and I checked out when we saw one of them sitting in a suspicious-looking white van," George said. "Somebody get some blankets. These boys look cold to me."

"We'll have to check those names out more when we get back to the station," Cody said.

One of the cops went to fetch the blankets, while the others began looking over the place for clues. They found evidence of cats being there with several kinds of cat hair on the floor, along with some cat feces and dried spots of cat urine.

"So if you were all tied up, how did you get loose?" Cody asked.

"It was Sam. We found a knife. He cut my rope with the knife while he was holding it with his teeth," said John. "Then I untied him."

"That was really good thinking on Sam's part," said George. "I can see he must have hurt his mouth a little bit."

"Yes, it did hurt some, but I had to get us loose. I just had to!" Sam exclaimed.

"Let me get a first aid kit, and we'll fix you right up," Cody told him. "Okay, somebody call my dad and Sergeant Phillips and let them know that we found the boys and we're bringing them in," he added.

One of the cops fetched a first aid kit from his car, and Cody applied some hydrogen peroxide to the sides of Sam's mouth, using a couple of cotton balls.

"We'll have a doctor check both of you out when we get back to town," he said.

Some of the detectives searched for fingerprints and found a couple on the wall near where the cages had been kept. Another one gathered samples of the cat hair, placing each color in a different bag.

Two more went back with flashlights to check out the generator and look for its serial number to see if they could trace when and where it was purchased.

"I guess that about wraps things up here," Cody said. "George, do you think our cruiser is drivable?"

George got in and tested the headlights. One of them was broken, but the other one worked. "I guess we can hobble back to town if we stay in line with our brothers," he said.

"Sure thing. We'll put you in the middle of our line," one of the cops agreed. "However, I don't want to be around when Sergeant Phillips sees your vehicle."

Everyone laughed sympathetically. One of them patted Cody on the back and shook his head. Cody rolled his eyes.

They all got into their vehicles and headed back to town. One of them had sent in the report that the boys had been found safe and sound but a little hungry.

Chapter 25

Word that the two boys had been found safe and unharmed spread quickly throughout the town, as it had been reported to the local news channel. Adolphus and Emma, along with Jonas and Eliza, were waiting at the hospital for the boys to arrive. They were too impatient to wait inside, so they were standing by the emergency entrance, along with some hospital personnel and Sergeant Phillips. A crowd had started to gather, so the sergeant called for backup to keep the crowd at bay.

"I think I see some flashing lights!" Emma announced.

"I hear some sirens," Adolphus added.

"I'll bet those boys are havin' the time of their lives ridin' in a police car with all of the excitement. I just hope they're okay," said Jonas.

Emma and Eliza held their breath as the line of cars rode by the emergency entrance with Cody and George's car pulling in beside the entrance door. Several nurses and other personnel were waiting with two stretchers. Someone opened the back door of the cruiser, and the two boys stepped out. Flashes went off as reporters began snapping pictures of the event. A live camera crew, along with a reporter from the local TV station, was waiting in the front of the crowd.

"How do you boys feel? Are you okay?" the reporter asked as a cameraman pointed the camera lens at them.

"We're fine. Just tired and hungry," Sam spoke for both of them.

The family rushed over to hug the boys, blocking the camera's view of their faces. The crowd began to cheer.

"This is Suzanne Antley reporting live from the Summerfield Memorial Hospital. The two boys who were kidnapped by the cat nabbers have been found and appear to be in good condition. A crowd has gathered to welcome them, and you can probably hear the cheers in the background. They are with their family now and are about to be wheeled into the hospital to be checked out. Further updates will be given when they become available. I'll turn it back over to our regular news crew back at the station now," she said, and the cameraman closed down the camera.

"If you two boys climb onto these stretchers, we'll take you to the ER to be checked out," one of the orderlies told them. The boys looked at each other and smiled before they followed his instructions. They were about to get another ride.

Meanwhile, Sergeant Phillips had not failed to notice that one of his cruisers was not in pristine condition. He walked over to Cody and George as the crowd began to disperse, and the family followed the boys through the emergency entrance.

"What's this I see? A broken headlight and a scratched front bumper on the cruiser?" he asked, frowning as he spoke.

"So sorry, Sergeant Phillips, but the boys were locked in an underground garage, and we couldn't pry the door open. We had to ram it with one of the vehicles," Cody told him.

"Well, having the boys back is more important than the cruiser," the sergeant admitted. "However, you men have a lot of paperwork to fill out. And what about the cats and the kidnappers? My wife's cat is still missing. She's not going to be happy about that."

"The team took some fingerprints and samples of cat hair that we found at the scene," George explained. The police are probably running the prints through the system now. Plus, we found out that the suspects go by the names Gus and Stan."

"Somebody definitely knew the area and knew about the deserted house in the woods," Cody told him. "Nobody's been there in years. We could barely find a place to park the police cars in what used to be the front yard. It's too bad because it used to be a beautiful place."

"Well, that's what happens when a person has no heirs," Sergeant Phillips commented. "Does it look like the house could be saved?"

"If somebody wanted to invest some money in it, there's still hope," Cody replied. "I know it's been up for sale several times, but the sales always fell through. My stepmom is friends with Linda Kay Spurgeon, the realtor who handled the transactions,. She told me that Linda Kay was pretty disappointed about not selling the place.

The sergeant looked back at the damaged car again and then looked at Cody and George.

"I guess cars can be repaired. I'm just glad those two boys are okay, but we still have to find those cats, not just for my wife, but for everybody else who lost them."

"Yes, and now that includes Miss Betty," Cody added.

"How is she doing, anyhow? Is there any improvement in her condition? The sergeant asked.

"No, she's still unconscious. The doctors are thinking about moving her to either a private room or maybe even a nursing home," said Cody with a touch of sadness in his voice.

"Go to the station and fill out your paperwork. I'll have one of the detectives interview the boys as soon as they've been checked out. Maybe we can get a clue about where the cats were headed," the sergeant instructed. "I'm going to speak to the families before I leave the hospital." He turned and walked through the emergency doors, leaving Cody and George to follow his instructions. They climbed back into the car with Cody driving.

"This is definitely not how I planned to spend my night," Cody commented as he maneuvered the car through the nighttime traffic and headed towards the station.

"Me either, but I'm sure glad we found those boys. It's too bad about the cats, but human life is always the most important thing," George responded.

"You're right; it certainly is. I think a lot of prayers were answered tonight when we found those boys. I said a few prayers myself," Cody told him.

"As did I," said George. "Our entire church was praying for their safe return."

"Let's get this paperwork done and fill out the report on the car. Then I have somebody I want to talk to," said Cody.

"I'll just bet you do!" George exclaimed. "The whole police department is talking about you and Jennifer. You took after your dad in your attitude about women, waiting so long to find the right woman, but I believe you finally found her."

"So do I, George. So do I, and I believe God had a hand in it all," Cody told him as they pulled into the police parking lot, exited the car, and headed inside to do the paperwork that awaited them.

Chapter 26

Gloria and Jennifer had held several consultations with the doctors about Miss Betty's condition. She wasn't any worse, but she wasn't any better, either. She was still unconscious and receiving intravenous medications. At times she seemed restless, moving her head from side to side and opening her mouth as if she were trying to speak.

Gloria and Jennifer both talked to her in soothing tones about her cats. They kept mentioning Toby's name in hopes that it would stir her enough to get her to open her eyes. They began taking turns reading to her from some of her favorite books, and soft music was playing in the background. The doctors had decided to move her to a private room rather than to a nursing home, and Gloria and Jennifer were grateful for that. They knew that the move to a nursing home might be the last one Miss Betty ever made.

"She's just got to wake up," Jennifer said worriedly one night as they sat in the room with her.

"If only Toby could be found. I think if we could bring him in here, it might stimulate her," Gloria said.

"Those cats have been missing for a few days now. If nobody is feeding and watering them, they might not make it," Jennifer observed.

"Well, whoever took them had a reason for doing it, so I'm sure they would want to keep the cats alive," said Gloria. "Let's just keep praying about it and for Miss Betty."

"You're right," Jennifer agreed. "Our church is still holding prayer vigils every night. Everybody loves Miss Betty so much."

They heard a soft knock on the door, and Jennifer rose to answer it. She was surprised to see Cody at such a late hour.

"Cody, why are you up so late?" she asked.

"I had a lot of paperwork to fill out, and I just finished it. How's Miss Betty?" he asked in a low tone.

"No better, I'm afraid. We are all praying for her. Did you have any luck in finding the cats? She needs Toby."

"Not yet, but the detectives and a lot of the police force are working on it. We got the possible names of the kidnappers from Jonas's great-nephews. That's something to go on. The police are running the names through the computer system now, along with a description of the men."

Gloria interrupted their conversation. "Excuse me, but I think I'll grab a cup of coffee and stretch my legs. You two can keep an eye on Miss Betty while I'm gone." She slipped out the door as Cody walked in.

"Come here, you," he said to Jennifer. "Do you know how much I've missed you?" He pulled her closer for a kiss.

She responded by putting her arms around his neck and kissing him back. Then she laid her head on his shoulder.

"Oh, Cody, I'm just so upset about everything. What if Toby and the other cats aren't found? I don't think Miss Betty will ever get over it, even if she regains consciousness, if Toby is gone forever."

"Remember when I told you to trust me?" he asked.

"Yes, I do."

"And what did you say?"

"I said I would always trust you, Cody," she replied.

"Well, just remember that promise. We're going to get those cats back and get Toby back to Miss Betty."

A tear trickled down Jennifer's cheek. She brushed it away with her hand. "I'm sorry to cry, but I just can't help it. I feel so helpless. I do trust you, Cody. I just hope you can find the cats in time."

He put his finger under her chin and tilted her face upwards to face him. "I am going to spend every waking minute looking for those cats." He kissed her again, and it seemed to comfort her. She was breathing easier now.

"I have to go now," he said. "I'm going back to the police station to see if there's any news about those kidnappers or the cats. I promise to let you know the minute I find out anything important."

She smiled at him, her tears gone for the moment. "Thank you so much," she whispered. She nodded towards the bed. "Miss Betty would thank you, too, if only she could."

"Don't worry. When we catch them, those kidnappers are going to be behind bars for a long time. Now, why don't you and your housemates get busy finishing the planning on that party? That should help take your mind off Miss Betty and the cats. After all, you are trying to help the feral cat program. Miss Betty would love that."

"Yes, she would. I'll speak with Gloria and go back home to check on the progress of the function. I don't know if we can really call it a party, but we hope to have a lot of fun activities. And don't forget—you promised to get all the police force there. At least, everybody who's not on duty at the time."

He realized that he was still holding her in his arms. He raised one hand and said, "I solemnly promise to get the police officers to your fundraising function." He touched her nose and gave her one last quick peck of a kiss.

"I have to go now," he told her as the door opened and Gloria re-entered the room.

"Did I miss anything?" she asked.

"Nothing I can report except that Cody has promised to get those cats back for us," Jennifer said.

"Hmmm…I see. Okay, then. Good seeing you again, Cody. Looks like you're leaving."

"Yes, I have to go now. Goodbye to both of you," he said as he exited the room.

Jennifer turned to Gloria and explained to her what she and Cody had discussed about the upcoming fundraising event. She ended with, "So, I hate to leave you alone, but I need to get home and consult with Donna and Laura so we can keep the wheels running on this thing we've started."

"Don't worry about me," Gloria told her. "I can doze off on this couch. I just want to be near Miss Betty in case she wakes up. She won't know what happened or why she's here. She needs me."

"Of course, she does. Just be sure to phone me if there's a change in her condition," said Jennifer as she gathered her purse and other supplies and prepared to leave. She hugged Gloria before she headed towards the door. She just hoped those housemates of hers hadn't slacked off on their duties while she had been spending time with Miss Betty.

Chapter 27

Jennifer arrived at home to find that her two housemates had already gone to bed. She didn't realize it was so late. She seemed to have lost all track of time since taking leave from her job at the fire department to sit with Miss Betty. It had been just a short time, but the days and nights had melded together into one long, continuous set of problems.

She sighed as she headed up the stairs. She would have to wait until tomorrow morning to talk to Donna and Laura. What she needed more than anything right now was a good night's sleep.

She awakened to the smell of bacon frying. Suddenly, she realized that she was hungry. She turned off her alarm and arose from bed, picking up her robe and putting it on as she headed for the stairs. She knew she could always count on her housemates to come through with food when it was needed.

She walked into the kitchen to find both of them busy preparing breakfast. They had even set the table for three, which meant that they had planned on her joining them.

"Jennifer, I see you're up," Donna said. "We didn't hear you come in last night."

"I spotted your car in the driveway, so we knew you were here," Laura explained. "That's why we set the table for three. We've got some news for you about our fundraising event."

"I can't wait to hear it," Jennifer told her. "I was beginning to get concerned."

"We've got the people in the local Humane Society helping us to sell tickets," said Donna.

"That's great!" Jennifer said enthusiastically. "I'm surprised you got the tickets and the flyers printed so quickly."

"Oh, I have a couple of connections with the town's printing company, and I told them it was a rush job," Donna replied.

"Yes, and the radio ads have started. All we need now is to plan the games and decorations," Laura added.

"Since Gloria insisted that I come home and work with you two, we can get started on it right after breakfast. What are we having because I'm starved?" Jennifer asked.

"We thought we would surprise you with bacon and waffles with strawberries," Laura told her. "Just so happens that we like that menu ourselves."

"So, when do we eat?" Jennifer inquired.

"Everything's ready, so help us get it on the table and we can start eating," Donna told her as she handed her a plate of steaming waffles.

Jennifer set the waffles on the table, while Laura brought in the bacon and strawberries. Donna poured the coffee before she sat down at the table, where the other two had already taken their seats. After a brief blessing for the food and a prayer for Miss Betty, they all began eating.

They made short work of finishing off the food and cleaning up the kitchen. Jennifer brought her laptop down from her room and put it on the table.

"So, let's see what fun things we can come up with for people of all ages," she said as she began searching for ideas on the computer.

After several hours of work, they decided that they had enough games and had ordered what they needed for the games plus the materials for the decorations. Laura and Donna had gotten the measurements of the main room of the Convention Center from the director. They felt that they were making a lot of headway.

Donna had brought several rolls of tickets home with her, along with a box of the flyers. The plan was for her and Laura to each take a roll of tickets to work with them the next day. They had both taken the day off to work on the fundraising event. They headed out to put up some flyers around town. Jennifer picked up some flyers and a roll of tickets and walked over to the house next door, where Cody's parents lived. She hoped she could convince Jillian to take them to school to sell.

Jillian answered the door quickly and invited Jennifer to come into the living room. Jennifer explained her mission and told Jillian about the upcoming fundraising event.

"Of course, I would be glad to take the flyers over to the elementary school for you, Jennifer. I still know most of the teachers there, even though I retired a couple of years ago. I still substitute teach once in a while if they need me," Jillian said. "If you have any tickets, I will take them and see if I can sell them to the faculty members."

"That would be wonderful," Jennifer told her. "I do appreciate your help so much."

She handed Jillian some flyers and twenty of the tickets, telling her how much they cost.

"You know, I've been hearing a lot about you from Cody these days. I think that he's quite taken with you," said Jillian as she took the materials from Jennifer.

Jennifer looked at her shyly, remembering the days when she was the student and Jillian was her teacher. She blushed slightly before she spoke.

"Yes, Cody and I have been seeing each other," she admitted. "It took us a while to come to an understanding, but we've fallen in love. It was a slow, but sure process."

"So, Cody takes after his dad in that way, too, I see. I'm not surprised. But take it from me. If you catch one of those Hawthorne men, you've got yourself quite a catch." She smiled as she spoke.

"Yes, you're right. I trust Cody totally, and he has promised to bring all those missing cats back home," Jennifer told her.

"I'm sure between Cody, his dad, and Sergeant Phillips, those men and the cats will be found," Jillian assured her.

"I'd better be off for now. I need to sell some of these tickets to those tricky firefighters I work with," Jennifer said as she rose to leave.

She walked back to her house and grabbed her purse and her car keys, along with the roll of tickets and headed to the firehouse.

She walked in with tickets in hand and was immediately greeted heartily by all the firefighters who were present.

"Jennifer, so great to see you again. When are you coming back to work?" asked Freddy.

"Yes, we're missing you and your cooking," said Calvin. "I can't take much more of the complaining when it's my turn to cook."

"Boy, do I have a treat for you!" Jennifer exclaimed. "How would you like to eat some really delicious food, have some fun, and meet some good-looking women?"

"Would I! If they can cook, I'm all in," said Calvin.

Jennifer began to explain her plan to the rest of the crew as they gathered around to listen. They were all interested, and every one of them bought at least one ticket. Some bought more because they had families. Before she knew it, she had sold over one-third of the roll.

"It all sounds great to me except for the part about meeting the women. Remember, I'm married," Don told her.

"Yes, and you have a lovely wife who can cook, so you're all set," Jennifer teased.

"Well, I'm not. Bring on the women and the food!" Calvin declared.

"I'll do just that," Jennifer promised. "Sorry guys, but I have to go now. I have a lot of things to do, and there's still Miss Betty to watch over."

"How is she?" asked Don.

"Still unconscious, I'm afraid," Jennifer replied.

"I'm sorry to hear that," said Don

"We have lots of prayer chains and prayer vigils going for her. Feel free to come to any church in town and join in," Jennifer announced, looking around at the entire group as she spoke.

"We'll be there, and we'll be at the fundraiser, too," Freddy assured her.

"That makes me very happy. You guys are so great to work with. I promise to be back working soon," Jennifer said as she gathered her materials and prepared to leave.

"Goodbye for now," she said as she walked outside and headed for her car.

Freddy stared at her thoughtfully as she walked out. "There's something different about our Jennifer. Did anybody else notice it?" he asked. "She has a glow about her, almost like a pregnant woman… you don't think…"

"No, not Jennifer," Don replied. "The girl's in love. I've seen that look before. It's how my wife looked when we first fell in love."

"Oh, no. If she gets married, there goes all of our good food," Calvin complained.

"I wouldn't worry about that," Don assured him. "There's no way she's giving up being the first female firefighter in the county. No way at all."

Chapter 28

The entire Summerfield police department had been devoting themselves to finding the missing cats and the two men who took them in the white van. Time was of the essence for the safety of the cats. Their computers had been working overtime and had come up with a match for the one Sam called "Gus." It seemed that he had a police record for petty theft and had done some jail time for several charges. Someone ran off a copy of his picture, and Cody took it, along with several other mug shots to see if the boys could identify him. Sam picked him out immediately.

"Yes, he's the one," Sam stated. "He seemed to be controlling the operation. The other guy was just his assistant."

"Thanks, Sam. You've been a big help," Cody told him. "We're working on this case day and night. I know we'll catch them soon."

"Okay, Mr. Cody. I hope you do because those are some mean men," Sam replied.

Cody left and returned to the department, where he informed his fellow officers that a definite identification had been made on one of the cat nabbers. Everyone cheered because they were one step closer to catching the criminals. Sergeant Phillips was especially happy because it meant that they might be one step closer to getting his wife's cat back, if it were possible that the cat was still alive.

"I just wonder how they pulled off those fake I.D.'s," said Cody. "They came up as legit on our computers."

"Yes, I had a check run on them, and no red flags popped up. They must be working for some real pros," George commented.

Chief Hawthorne instructed the detectives to extend their search for the van to neighboring regions as it has not been spotted in any of the surrounding counties or anywhere else in the state. They worked diligently, contacting police departments in various cities, and at last, they came upon a piece of information that proved to be helpful. Someone in another state had complained about a white van being parked under a large tree on their property, which was located in a rural area.

The local police there rushed to the scene and found the van with its windows open. The van was filled with cages of cats, many of them in bad condition from heat and dehydration. They called their local Humane Society, which hurried to the scene with their rescue vans and several veterinarians to help them. They began to remove the cats from the van and immediately began to administer aid to them, supplying water to those who could drink it and IV's to those who were too weak to respond. Several of the cats in the bottom cages were dead.

The police dusted the van for fingerprints, and some of them proved to be a match for one of the suspects. They were closing in on the cruel men who had deprived so many families of their beloved pets. An APB was issued for Gus, whose last name was listed as "Jones," although he appeared to have several other aliases.

Phone calls came in from people who had seen Gus and another man walking along the road where the van was found. They were seen attempting to hitch a ride, and someone evidently picked them up. Their whereabouts was currently unknown.

The police in the area where the van was found notified the Summerfield police department that the cats had been located and were currently under the care of their Humane Society. They would be transported back to Summerfield as soon as they were able to travel.

Sergeant Phillips was happy to get the news about the cats being found, and he immediately began to inquire about the appearance of the cats to see if any of them matched the description of his wife's cat. One of the Humane Society workers sent him several pictures taken with her phone, and he was relieved to see that his wife's cat was among those who survived the rescue.

"Now I don't have to sleep on the couch anymore," he told his staff. "I don't think my back could have taken many more nights of that torture! I'm just sorry that some of the cats didn't make it."

Cody called Jennifer and informed her that the cats had been found. He was still trying to find out if Miss Betty's cats were among the survivors. He assured her that he would let her know as soon as he could.

"Oh, Cody, I'm so happy that the cats have been found, but what about the men who took them and also kidnapped the boys?" she asked.

"We're still looking for the two men," he told her. "We'll get them yet. They won't escape the wrath of Sergeant Phillips. I almost feel sorry for them."

"When will the cats come home?" she asked.

"Some of them were in pretty bad shape, but we're working with the Humane Society here to set up a time where people can come with pictures of their cats to claim them. Some of them are feral. That's probably why we didn't catch any on our last outing," he said.

"I have an idea," she told him. "Why don't we combine the returning of the cats with our fund-raising event? The cats should be well by then. Everybody would be happy, and we would probably get some extra donations."

"Say, that's a good idea," he agreed. "Why don't you add that to the advertisement and see if you can get a news story on TV about it?"

"I'll do just that!" she exclaimed. "I'm getting pretty excited about this fundraising event. I think we'll have to call it a party now."

"Yes, definitely," he said. "There will be a lot of happy people there. Some of them might adopt some of the unclaimed cats, too."

"You're right, but remember, most feral cats can't be adopted. I think we need to find out who has been feeding them, and maybe they can identify some of them and we can return them to their original surroundings. Of course, they need to be checked for the TNR program first."

"Yes, that's the best thing to do," he agreed. "You talk to Donna and Laura and get everything set. The cats will be coming back soon."

"Okay, I'll do that. Thanks so much for letting me know. I'll tell Gloria. If only Miss Betty would wake up. Then everything would be wonderful."

"Just keep praying about it. God will find a way," he told her.

"You're right. We'll keep up the prayer chains and prayer vigils," she said.

Chapter 29

Jennifer had decided to continue her leave from the fire department until after the TNR fundraising event was held. She, along with Donna and Laura, was totally occupied with the ticket sales, advertising, and getting everything set up with the decorations and the games and fun activities. Fortunately, the Summerfield Humane Society was still helping with the ticket sales, and they had some volunteers from several churches to help them get everything ready for the party.

Jennifer was giddy with excitement. "I can't believe everything is going so well. I'm so glad the people let us have the Convention Hall for two days to get everything set up," she told Donna and Laura.

"Girl, you are the star of the event. You thought it up, and you came up with the ideas. The highlight will be when the people are reunited with their cats," said Donna.

"Yes, we're so lucky to get most of them back. I think the ones who died were ferals. I'm hoping all the family cats will soon be back with their owners," Jennifer commented. "They are being transported here in a climate-controlled truck sponsored by the local Humane Society."

"It's great the way you arranged everything once Cody set everything in motion for the cats to come back to Summerfield," Laura noted.

"Yes, some are still recovering. They being taken to Summerfield's Humane Society headquarters, but it's very crowded. They really need a place with more room. However, they're always short of money," said Jennifer.

"Too bad somebody doesn't donate a bigger place to them." Donna offered her opinion on the matter.

"That would be the icing on the cake, but not many people would be willing to do that," Jennifer observed. "Let's just take it one step at a time and see what happens."

"The best thing to happen would be if Miss Betty wakes up and sees all of this," Laura said.

"You're right. I'm still praying for her. She's hung on this long. We can't lose her now. Cody and I have a plan."

"Really? What is it?" asked Laura.

"Cody managed to get Miss Betty's cats separated from the rest. He gave them to Gloria, and she's been keeping them at Miss Betty's house. They've just about recovered from their traumatic experiences. I don't think any of them will ever want to go outside again," Jennifer told them.

"So, no more Toby climbing the trees, huh?" Donna teased.

"There's no need for it now. Miss Betty was just trying to get me and Cody together, and it worked. We're a real couple now."

"But we're still looking," Laura complained.

"Remember, we have all of those firefighters and police officers coming to the event. A lot of them are single, so doll yourselves up and see what happens," Jennifer told them.

"Oh, we can do that," Donna assured her. "I just hope I don't have as much trouble picking out a dress to wear as you did."

They all laughed at that comment, remembering the pile of dresses stacked on Jennifer's bed before her date with Cody.

"I'm sure you'll both be fine," said Jennifer.

Cody had been busy with both his police duties and the cat rescue. His dad had put him in charge of getting the cats back to Summerfield and into some kind of shelter. He had lucked out when the local Humane Society stepped in and gave him a helping hand. In addition to transporting the cats back to Summerfield, they had made room for all the cats at their crowded shelter. The shelter was nice, but way too small for their needs, he had decided.

It was then that an idea came to him. He remembered the deserted house where the boys had been held. It was roomy enough, and his stepmom was in the same Bible study class as Linda Kay Spurgeon, the realtor who still held the title to it. He wondered if something could be worked out seeing as how she had been unable to sell it. He talked to Jillian, and she promised to speak to Linda Kay about the house.

He was also excited about the upcoming fundraising party. Yes, it had turned into a party, not just "an event" now. The whole town was celebrating the return of the kidnapped boys and the hapless cats. Plus, the families were glad that they would be getting their pets back. He had one extra surprise for Jennifer. He just hoped it would be as happy an event as the party.

Gloria called Jennifer a week before the fundraising party. "I have an idea," she said.

"What is it?" Jennifer asked.

"Why don't you and Cody meet me at the hospital tonight about 7 p.m.? I'll show you then," she said.

"Okay, we'll be there," Jennifer promised. She called Cody as soon as she hung up the other call, and he agreed to pick her up at her house to go to the hospital.

"I wonder what Gloria has planned," he commented as he and Jennifer drove to the hospital.

"I don't know, but it must be important if she wants both of us there. Look, there's her car now," Jennifer said as they pulled into the hospital parking lot.

Gloria stepped out of her car and walked to the passenger side and picked up what appeared to be a cat comfort carrier. They could see Toby's face peeking out of the front.

They quickly exited their vehicle and walked over to Gloria.

"I can't believe you got Toby out of the house," Jennifer said.

"Oh, he just loves this type of cat carrier. It's the latest thing," Gloria told her. "So, remember that I kept saying what Miss Betty needed was Toby?"

"Yes, I remember," Jennifer replied.

"I'm going to try something with the permission of the hospital. I'm going to take Toby and put him in Miss Betty's bed and see if there's any reaction on her part. I know Toby will be glad to see her. All of the cats have been wandering around the house looking for her. They're just lost without their mistress."

"That's a good idea," Cody commented. "I think it just might work."

"I wanted you two here because next to the cats, you are the second thing she was thinking about before the kidnapping incident. She'll be so happy to see you together."

"What are we waiting for?" Jennifer asked. "Let's see if our prayers have been answered.

They walked quietly into Miss Betty's dimly lit room. The soft music was still playing. Miss Betty looked peaceful, but still had not opened her eyes. Gloria took Toby out of the carrier and placed him at the foot of Miss Betty's bed. He looked around and then headed straight for the head of the bed and lay down beside Miss Betty, purring loudly and rubbing his head against her shoulder.

"Is it working?" Jennifer whispered.

"Give it time," Gloria replied. "Let Miss Betty hear those purrs. She loved it when Toby was in her lap purring."

Miss Betty stirred slightly. They all held their breath to see what would happen next. Her eyelids fluttered and then opened and closed several times. Her hand moved towards Toby until she could feel his fur. Suddenly, she was awake and staring at the cat that was lying contentedly beside her.

"Toby," she whispered. "Toby."

"I'm calling the nurse," said Gloria.

Cody put his arm around Jennifer and pulled her close to him.

Miss Betty's eyes shifted towards the couple. She smiled slightly.

"Miss Betty, you're awake," said Jennifer.

Miss Betty managed to give a slight nod just as a nurse entered the room.

"Well, wonder of wonders! Our star patient is awake," the nurse exclaimed. "Just let me check your vitals and then I'll notify the doctor."

Miss Betty was very still as the nurse performed her duties. "We're all good," the nurse told them. "Her temperature, heart rate, and blood pressure have returned to normal. The doctor will be so happy. He's been by every day to check on her. Sometimes more than once a day."

Miss Betty whispered, "No worry. Toby's here."

"Yes, Miss Betty. I knew that was just what you needed," Gloria told her. "Hallelujah! A lot of prayers have been answered tonight. Do you know the whole town has been praying for your recovery?"

"No," Miss Betty whispered. "I'm glad."

"Well, don't you worry," Cody told her. "We got the cats back, and we're looking for those bad men who tied you up."

"You fell over and hit your head," Gloria explained. "You've been in a coma for over a month."

"Don't remember…," Miss Betty said, her voice growing a little stronger.

"It doesn't matter," Jennifer told her. "We're having a big fundraising event and a May Day celebration for the TNR program."

Miss Betty smiled. "Knew you could do it…," her voice trailed off.

"We're going to go now, Miss Betty," Cody said. "We don't want to tire you out. The doctor should be here soon to check on you."

Miss Betty smiled weakly and half-raised her hand. "Bye," she whispered.

"I'll stay here with her and Toby. You two had better scoot. I know you still have a lot to do," Gloria told them.

"Goodbye, Miss Betty," they said in unison as they exited the door. Cody closed it softly behind them.

"You know, I have an idea," Jennifer told Cody as they walked back towards his truck.

"What is it?" Cody asked.

"Why don't we set up some cameras at the Convention Center and put a laptop in Miss Betty's room, and she can watch the fundraising party?"

"That's a great idea!" Cody agreed. "I can have some of the police techs set it up. I think Miss Betty will love it, and that will help her to recover faster. I'll get right on it as soon as I get back to the department."

Chapter 30

Things moved along at a rapid pace with the date for the fundraising event fast approaching. Jennifer, Donna, and Laura had all been working on getting everything set up, along with some volunteers from several churches. All of the tickets had been sold. A place was set up for the band to perform, and the room for the cats was ready.

Miss Betty was still in the hospital, but she had begun physical therapy on learning how to walk again after being in a coma for so long. Her appetite had returned, although she complained about the hospital food. Gloria managed to sneak her some home-cooked food several times, and she had eaten every bite of it. Toby was still with her. Gloria had set up a litter box and feeding station in one corner of the room. Miss Betty complained about not being able to see Orphan Annie and Snowball, but Gloria recorded some videos of them at Miss Betty's home and showed the videos to her. That seemed to satisfy her for the time being.

Just before the day of the fundraising event, several men showed up and set up the computer in her room so she could view everything taking place. Both she and Gloria were getting excited about it. She gave Gloria one special assignment that was a secret just between them. Nobody was to know about it until the party took place.

On the day of the party, Jennifer and her two housemates were all jitters. It was hard to tell which one of them was more nervous. Jennifer was anxious because she had been selected to preside over the event and make the announcements and give a speech. Donna and Laura were edgy because they were hoping to meet some eligible bachelors and brighten up their love life. All three were trying to decide what to wear.

"Oh, let's not get ourselves into a pickle again about picking out the right clothes to wear," Jennifer told them. "We all have plenty of clothes to choose from, and we all look good when we're dressed up, so head to your closets and find the right outfits."

All of them went to their rooms and began to search through their wardrobes. Donna ended up with a yellow dress that set off her strawberry blonde hair and green eyes. Laura chose a blue dress that complemented her brown hair and brought out the blue in her eyes. Jennifer chose a green dress, just to be different. They all applied their makeup carefully and fixed each other's hair before donning the dresses. They decided that shoes with lower heels would be the best, as they would be standing most of the time.

They rode to the Convention Center in Jennifer's car to save parking spaces. Cody had offered to pick Jennifer up, but she needed to get there early to oversee the final details of getting everything ready. They walked into the center and were amazed at what a wonderful transformation had taken place from an empty room to one filled with all kinds of booths and decorations of balloons and signs made by some of the school children, along with crepe paper hanging around the edges of the ceiling.

Jennifer took a peek at the room where the cats waited in their cages with several people assigned to watch over them and a table set up for people to show pictures of their pets and sign a release form. There were also papers for people who might want to adopt some of the unclaimed cats.

The stage had been set up for the band, along with microphones for the people who would be speaking. A table with chairs was at the entrance for several people to collect tickets and also money for people to pay if they had no tickets. Jennifer just hoped that everybody could fit into the room, but speakers and a big-screen TV had been set up outside in case of an overflow crowd. She couldn't think of anything that had been left out.

Cody drove up shortly after the women arrived to see if there was anything he could do to help. He noted that everything seemed to be under control. He patted his pocket that contained a bulge with a small box in it. He hoped nobody would notice until the right time came for his surprise for Jennifer.

In a short time, the place was filled with people of all ages. The children were enjoying the games, along with some popcorn and cotton candy at the booths in several rooms. The adults were sampling cookies, sandwiches, and a variety of soft drinks that had been donated by Rosalena's restaurant.

People were mixing and mingling on the floor of the largest room, but one section in front of the stage had been roped off with a Maypole in the center. Decorative colored streamers were hanging from the poles awaiting a Maypole dance to be performed by Miss Shelly's Dance Studio of young children. They were lining up, about to begin their performance. People began to gather round to watch the dance. Jennifer stepped up to the microphone on the stage and announced that it was time to begin the ceremonies. The band began playing, and the dancers wasted no time in going into the routine they had rehearsed.

Once the colorful Maypole had been wound, they received a hearty round of applause, with their parents being the most enthusiastic fans. The Maypole was then wheeled off to the side to make room for more dancing by the adults.

Both the police force and the firefighters not on duty showed up in droves. Laura and Donna were looking them over as prospects for future dates. Jennifer introduced the eligible firemen to them, and Donna paired off with Calvin for a dance. Laura ended up dancing with one of the policemen who had been introduced to her by Cody.

Cody and Jennifer were dancing and watching the events unfolding. It looked like Donna and Laura might both be getting their wishes granted to meet eligible men. A lot of other couples were also dancing, giving a festive look to the event.

"I hope Miss Betty is watching," Jennifer commented as she and Cody made their way around the dance floor. "Maybe I should call Gloria and check."

"You don't have to," Cody told her. "I already had one of the men check, and Gloria reported that the reception is working fine and Miss Betty is having the time of her life."

"I'm so glad. Especially after all she's gone through," Jennifer said. "It will be so good to have her home again."

"Yes, let's hope it won't be long," Cody added.

It was time for Jennifer to make her formal speech, so they worked their way towards the stage. The band stopped playing as Jennifer climbed the stairs to the stage. She approached the microphone and began to talk.

"Thank you all for coming tonight," she said. "I'm happy to report that the fundraising has been a success, and we now have a great nest egg for the TNR program, along with some money donated to the

Summerfield Humane Society. They need to enlarge their space, and this money will help with that."

Everyone clapped, and Cody climbed the stairs and approached the microphone. Jennifer looked at him with surprise. He wasn't supposed to be making a speech.

"I have something to add to that," he said as he stepped up to the microphone. "There has been another donation that will help the whole community, as well as the local Humane Society. Several donors who wish to remain anonymous have bought a new home for Summerfield's Humane Society. It's the old Harris house located outside of town. It needs a lot of work, but the materials to fix it up have also been donated. What we are going to need is lots of volunteers to do the work. When it's finished, there will be room for both cats and dogs to stay permanently. It will be a 'no kill shelter.' The Humane Society will still have their headquarters downtown where people can come and pick out animals to adopt. The name of the new center will be The Betty Applewhite Animal Shelter in honor of Miss Betty Applewhite, who has done so much to rescue and help homeless animals over the years." The crowd clapped and cheered, along with a few whistles thrown in for good measure.

Jennifer took a step back because her eyes teared up again after hearing the announcement. She wished she could see the look on Miss Betty's face now. She also wished she had a tissue or something to blot her eyes with. Cody pulled a handkerchief out of his pocket and handed it to her.

Before either one of them could say anything else, Gloria appeared at the edge of the stage. She was holding something close to her chest. She climbed the stairs to the stage and approached the microphone. Cody stepped back to let her speak.

"Most of you know me," she said. "I'm Gloria Howard. I've been

Miss Betty's caretaker for a number of years. I would like to report that Miss Betty is just fine and will be home in a few days."

The crowd began clapping and cheering again, interrupting the speech. Gloria paused until it all died down. Then she continued. "Miss Betty is watching, and she thanks everyone for all the hard work you did. She will be honored to have the new shelter named after her. But she sent something special to this event, and it's something for Jennifer Clark, who has been heading up the TNR program for the past few months."

She then held out what she had been hiding close to her chest. It was a tiny, gray-striped tabby kitten wrapped in a small towel. "Jennifer, this is for you," she said.

"Oh, how cute," Jennifer said, as she held out her hands for the kitten, which was trembling slightly. "Does it have a name?"

"Miss Betty named him Boo," Gloria replied.

"Boo--a perfect name," Jennifer agreed as she gently clutched the kitten to her chest. "Thank you. I promise to love him and take care of him always."

Everyone applauded, showing their approval. They were a jovial crowd. Some of the children jumped up and down, waving their arms.

Cody stepped up to the microphone as Gloria stepped back. "There's one more thing I have to say. I'm taking a real chance here, but bear with me."

He pulled a box from his pocket and opened it to reveal a sparkling diamond ring. He got down on one knee and faced Jennifer, who was still clutching the kitten to her chest. A silence fell over the crowd, as he now had everyone's full attention.

"Jennifer, I love you with all my heart. I hope you feel the same way about me. Will you marry me?" he asked as he held out the ring box.

Jennifer looked at him with love in her eyes. "This night has so many surprises. It's so hard for me to take in," she said. She stepped forward, and Cody took her hand.

"Yes, I'll marry you, Cody," she told him.

Cheers and whistles were heard as he slipped the ring on her finger. She held the kitten with her right hand. He stood and kissed her soundly.

"Champagne," someone shouted, leading everyone else to laugh.

Their laughter was interrupted as Sergeant Phillips climbed to the stage. It was hard to read the expression on his face. Nobody ever knew what kind of mood he might be in. Jennifer and Cody stepped back to give him access to the microphone.

"I have an announcement to make," he said. "I just got word that both of the catnabbers/kidnappers have been apprehended. They tried to hold up a convenience store in another state. We found out that they were kidnapping the cats to sell them for medical experiments. Their van quit working, so they deserted the cats and left them in the van under a large shade tree with the front windows open, hoping to come back for them later. Fortunately, the van was spotted before it had been there very long."

The crowd began clapping once again.

Jennifer stepped to the microphone, after having regained her composure. Cody stood by her side for moral support.

"Now comes the moment we've all been waiting for," she said. "It's time for the cat owners to be reunited with their cats. Plus, there's a chance for anyone else to put in for adoption for the unclaimed cats that are here tonight. There are still some at the shelter who didn't match up with an owner, so you may go there any time if you're still interested."

The crowd dispersed and headed towards the room where the cats were located. Two policemen were on duty to keep order and keep the room from becoming overcrowded.

"It's going to take a while for all of those people to claim their cats," Cody noted.

"Yes, but they won't mind waiting. They've waited this long. Everyone will be happy," said Jennifer.

"Not as happy as you've made me," he told her. "There's just one catch."

"What's that?" she asked.

"Those two housemates of yours are going to have to find a new place to live because I want us to live in my stepmom's house right next to my family."

Jennifer scanned the crowd, looking for Donna and Laura. Both were engrossed in conversation with their dance partners.

"Oh, I don't think you'll have anything to worry about. Looks like those two might be moving out soon anyhow," she said.

The band began playing dance music again, and some of the couples re-entered the dance floor. Children were dancing around the outer edges of the rope.

"How about another dance?" he asked.

"We can't squash Boo," she told him.

"I promise to be gentle," he said as they headed towards the dance floor.

"You know what I just remembered?" she asked.

"No, what?" he responded.

"I never did get that Saturday night dinner."

Cody laughed. "There will be plenty of Saturday night dinners for us for the rest of our lives," he promised as he bent down carefully to give her another kiss.

THE END

Lagniappe

My family has always been animal lovers, especially my mom, who was never without a pet, even when she was growing up. I would like to share with you some of the pictures of our pets and the poems I wrote about them.

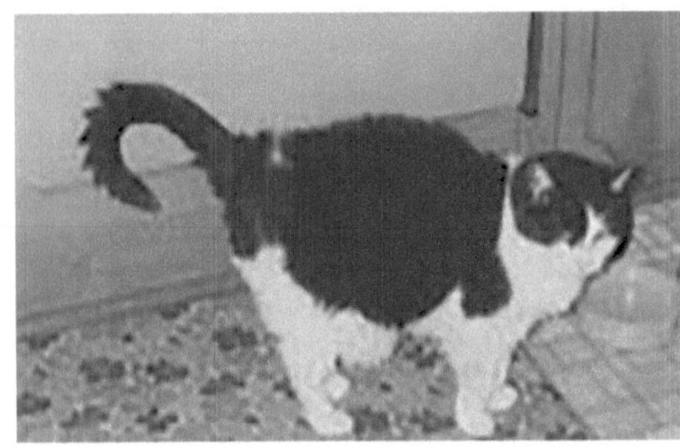

Orphan Annie

Snowball

Boo

My mom and her cat, 1918.

My sister and her
cat, Confucius
("Fu"), 1965

"Annie"

Written by Dianne H. Lundy

"Orphan Annie" was her name;
Riding out a storm she came
From her secret hiding place
Towards a warm and friendly face.

Tossed aside without a care,
Cold and scared she lingered there
Until at last all safe from harm,
She found a pair of loving arms.

A bowl of milk, a tender pat,
The kitten grew into a cat
With shiny fur of black and white
And eyes of green so wide and bright.

As years passed by their friendship grew,
And finally just the two
Were left to dwell on times gone by
When friends and loved ones lingered nigh.

At the end of eighteen years
Her mistress died amid the tears
Of loving girls who promised that
They would not forget the cat.

At her second home she found
A place to rest and settle down
And also time to run and play
With other cats who came her way.

There she finished out her life
In carefree style away from strife.
When at last her time was done,
She reached the age of twenty-one.

"Snowball

Written by Dianne H. Lundy

Snowball never learned her name,
So just plain "Kitty" she became
With bright green eyes and snow white fur,
A soft meow but quite a purr.

When she was only eight weeks old,
All alone out in the cold,
There in the bushes she was seen
On just one day past Halloween.

A little boy yearned for a pet,
So a new home she would get,
Where lots of love was soon bestowed
On one small cat, no longer cold.

For many years she shared her space
With hamsters, birds, and fish,
Until at last one fateful day,
She finally got her wish.

When, all according to God's plan,
Another cat then joined the clan.
Not waiting to be hugged or fed,
She headed straight for Snowball's bed.

On guard at first, they hissed and spat,
Each swatting at the other cat,
'Til it was clear no one would win,
So they decided to be friends.

At morning time they ran and played,
Hide-and-seek or games of chase;
Then tired at last they stopped to rest,
Contentedly in separate beds.

Their good times all came to an end
When Snowball finally lost her friend,
Who died at age twenty-one,
Leaving Snowball all alone.

An aging cat with wiser ways,
In the autumn of her days,
She naps and dreams now and then
Of happy times with her old friend.